The Great Brain

DIAL BOOKS FOR YOUNG READERS

NEW YORK

The Great Brain

ILLUSTRATED BY MERCER MAYER

By John D. Fitzgerald

Library of Congress Catalog Card Number: 67–22252

ISBN 0-8037-3074-8 ISBN 0-8037-3076-4 (lib. bdg.)
Printed in the United States of America
Designed by The Etheredges
C O B E   20 19 18 17 16 15 14 13 12

For Michele Ann and John Michael

Contents

The Great Brain

The Magic Water Closet

MOST EVERYONE IN UTAH remembers 1896 as the year the territory became a state. But in Adenville it was celebrated by all the kids in town and by Papa and Mamma as the time of The Great Brain's reformation.

I was seven years old going on eight. Tom was ten, and my other brother, Sweyn, would soon be twelve. We were all born and raised in Adenville, which was a typical Utah town with big wide streets lined with trees that had been planted by the early Mormon pioneers.

Adenville had a population of twenty-five hundred people, of which about two thousand were Mormons and the rest Catholics and Protestants. Mormons and non-Mormons had

1

learned to live together with some degree of tolerance and understanding by that time. But tolerance hadn't come easy for my oldest brother, Sweyn, my brother Tom, and myself. Most of our playmates were Mormon kids, but we taught them tolerance. It was just a question of us all learning how to fight good enough for Sweyn to whip every Mormon kid his age, Tom to whip every Mormon kid his age, and for me to whip every Mormon kid my age in town. After all, there is nothing as tolerant and understanding as a kid you can whip.

We never had any really cold weather or snow in Adenville because it was situated in the southwestern part of Utah, known to the Mormons as Dixie due to its mild climate. This was fortunate since we didn't have indoor toilets then. Everybody in town—from Calvin Whitlock, the banker, down—had to use a backhouse until the water closet Papa ordered arrived from Sears Roebuck. We called them backhouses and not outhouses because in Utah an outhouse was a sort of toolshed and storage room. Backhouses ran from two-holers to six-holers. Ours was a standard four-holer. You could just about judge a family's station in life by their backhouse. Just by looking at the Whitlock backhouse, with its ornate scroll woodwork trim and its fancy vent, you knew Calvin Whitlock was a person of means and influence in the community.

If there was one man in all of Adenville who would order the first water closet ever seen in town, that man had to be Papa. I thought Papa was the greatest man in the world except for one weakness. Papa just couldn't resist ordering any new invention that he saw advertised in magazines or catalogs. Our big attic was filled with crazy inventions that didn't work. Papa was always threatening to write to the presidents of these companies and denounce them as swindlers, but he never did. I guess he was afraid they would write back and call him a fool for believing what they said in their advertisements. Papa was editor and publisher of the *Adenville Weekly Advocate*. You would think a man smart enough to be an editor and publisher would be smart enough not to let himself be swindled. But Papa kept right on ordering new inventions. It was no surprise to anybody in town when they learned Papa had ordered the first water closet most people had ever seen.

The first Tom and I knew of it was the morning Fred Harvey walked into our backyard with a pick and shovel on his shoulder. He was the only plumber in town. He was a middle-aged man with a face that looked as if he'd just taken a bite out of a sour pickle. He was known as a very cranky person who didn't like kids. Mamma said the reason Mr. Harvey didn't like kids was because he had never had to put up with any of his own. It didn't sound quite right to me, but that is what Mamma said.

When Mr. Harvey came into our backyard, Tom and I were on our big back porch which ran the width of our house. We were beating with sticks on Mamma's washtubs, pretending that we were drummers in a band. Tom had a grin on his freckled face as he banged away. He was the only one in our family who had freckles. Tom didn't look like Papa and he didn't look like Mamma, unless you put them together. Then you could see that his hair was a cross between Papa's dark hair and Mamma's blond hair and that he had Papa's nose and mouth and Mamma's stubborn chin. Where the freckles came from was a mystery. I took after Papa and had curly black hair and dark eyes. My other brother, Sweyn, took after the Danish grandfather for whom he was named. He had blond hair and a stubborn Danish chin.

Tom and I heard the clanking sound of the pick and shovel being dropped to the ground by Mr. Harvey over the sound of our beating on the washtubs. We stopped and turned around to watch.

Mr. Harvey pulled a bandanna handkerchief from his overalls' pocket and blew his nose loudly. Then he looked at us as if he resented us being on our own back porch.

"Why aren't you kids in school?" he demanded.

"Because there isn't any school today," Tom said, glaring right back at Mr. Harvey. "And there might not be any school for a whole week."

"And why not?" Mr. Harvey asked.

"Because Miss Thatcher is sick," Tom answered.

Mr. Harvey certainly knew that Miss Thatcher taught the first through the sixth grades in our one-room schoolhouse. He also knew that when she was sick there wasn't any school for any kid in town. I guess this kind of upset him.

"If I'd known that," he said as if angry, "I wouldn't have taken this job."

Tom and I watched Mr. Harvey start to dig a hole in our backyard.

"What is he doing?" I asked, just as curious as I could be.

"Let's find out," Tom said.

We left the porch and approached Mr. Harvey.

"Why are you digging a hole?" Tom asked, polite as all get out.

"To bury nosy little boys in," Mr. Harvey said gruffly. "Now get away from me and leave me to my work."

"Come on, J.D.," Tom said, heading back for the porch. "We'll ask Mamma."

4

My brothers and I always called each other by our initials because that was the way Papa addressed us. We all had the same middle initial because we all had the same middle name of Dennis, just like Papa. More than two hundred years before I was born, an ancestor of ours named Dennis betrayed six of his cousins to the English during the rebellion in County Meath, Ireland. His father decreed that all male Fitzgeralds must bear the middle name of Dennis to remind them of the cowardice of his son.

I followed Tom into our big kitchen with its ten-foot-wide coal-burning range. Mamma was kneading dough on the big kitchen table as we entered. I had never seen Mamma's hands idle. They were busy hands—sewing, mending, cooking, washing, knitting, and always moving.

Mamma's blond hair was piled high in braids on her head. The sunshine coming through the kitchen window and striking Mamma's head made her hair look like golden sunlight.

She looked at us and smiled. "What have you two boys on your minds?" she asked.

"Why is Mr. Harvey digging a hole in our backyard?" Tom asked.

"It is the cesspool for the water closet your father ordered from Sears Roebuck," Mamma answered.

Aunt Bertha, who had lived with us since the death of her husband, was greasing a bread pan with bacon rinds. She wasn't really our aunt, but we called her Aunt Bertha because she was just like one of the family.

"This water closet business is the most foolish thing your husband ever did," she said to Mamma. When Aunt Bertha criticized Papa, he was always Mamma's "husband." When Papa did something Aunt Bertha approved of, he became "that man of ours." She was a big woman, with hands and feet like a man's and gray hair she always wore in a bun at the nape of her neck.

Tom scratched his freckled nose as wrinkles appeared on his high forehead. "You put china in a china closet," he said slowly. "You put clothes in a clothes closet. You put linen in a linen closet. But how can you put water in a water closet?"

I was dumbfounded. It was the first time in my life I'd ever heard my brother, with his great brain, admit he didn't know everything. Every year when Papa renewed his subscription to the *New York World,* they sent him *The World Almanac.* While Sweyn and I read books like *Black Beauty* and *Huckleberry Finn,* Tom read *The World Almanac* and the set of encyclopedias in our bookcase. Tom said his great brain had to know everything.

"A water closet is a toilet you have inside your house," Mamma explained. "That is why your father had Mr. Jamison partition off that room in the bathroom. The hole Mr. Harvey is digging is the cesspool for the new water closet."

"But Mamma," I protested, thinking about the odor coming from our backhouse, especially on hot days, "it will stink up the whole house."

Aunt Bertha agreed with me. "I tell you, Tena," she said to Mamma, "this is going to make us the laughing stock of Adenville."

"Now, Bertha," Mamma said with soft rebuke, "I've seen water closets in hotels in Salt Lake City and in Denver while on my honeymoon. I assure you they are very convenient and sanitary."

I remembered how I couldn't believe you could get water without a pump until they built the Adenville reser-

6

voir and Papa had explained how the reservoir being on higher ground forced the water through the pipes. And when Mr. Harvey had installed our hot-water heater and we got hot water right out of a tap, I thought it a miracle. But a backhouse in our bathroom was beyond my wildest imagination. I was positive that Papa had been swindled again on another crazy invention.

Tom and I went back outside to the porch. We watched as Mr. Harvey continued to dig the cesspool. In a little while Sammy Leeds, Danny Forester, and Andy Anderson came into our backyard. Mr. Harvey chased them away and told them to stay out of the backyard while he was working. Tom and I sat on the porch, watching until lunchtime.

Papa came home for lunch with Sweyn, who had been helping at the newspaper office. Mr. Harvey came to our back door. He demanded that Papa keep all kids out of the backyard while he was working. Papa told Sweyn to remain home to see that this was done.

"Can we watch from the back porch?" Tom asked.

"Yes," Papa agreed, "but stay out of the yard."

I could tell from the conniving look on Tom's face during lunch that his great brain was working like sixty to turn this to his financial advantage. He disappeared right after lunch. I went out to the back porch with Sweyn.

Mr. Harvey had just finished eating his own lunch which he had brought in a shoebox. He went to the hydrant and got a drink of water and then went to work. Mamma had asked him to have lunch with us, but Mr. Harvey had refused.

Sweyn and I sat on the railing of the back porch watching.

"Think you'll have any fights keeping the kids out of the backyard?" I asked hopefully.

7

"There is nobody left to fight," Sweyn said as if he regretted it.

"Maybe when Papa and Mamma send you to Salt Lake City to school next fall, you'll find some kids there to fight," I said, wanting to cheer him up.

He shook his head sadly. "It's a Catholic academy, J.D., and I don't believe the sisters or priests who teach there will allow any fighting."

I thought ahead to the time when I would be graduating from the sixth grade in Adenville like Sweyn would in June of that year. I too would be sent to school in Salt Lake City. The thought scared me and made my mouth dry. I went in to the kitchen to get a drink of water, just as the door leading to our side porch was thrust open. I stared bug-eyed as I watched Tom come through the hallway that separated our kitchen and dining room, followed by ten kids.

"It is all right, Mamma," Tom said as if he led ten kids into our kitchen every day. "Papa ordered Sweyn to keep the kids out of the backyard while Mr. Harvey is digging. But Papa said it was all right to watch from the porch. We can't get to the back porch without going into the backyard unless we go through the kitchen."

Aunt Bertha shook her head. "I tell you, Tena, that boy could talk his way around anything."

"He gets it from his father," Mamma said as if she was proud of Tom instead of angry with him for marching ten kids across her clean kitchen floor.

I couldn't believe my eyes as I watched Mamma go into the pantry and return with a big crock jar filled with cookies. She stationed herself near the door leading to the back porch.

"All right, boys," she said, smiling, "help yourselves to an oatmeal cookie as you pass by."

I had to fall in line last to get one of my own mother's cookies. Tom was munching on his cookie as I joined him on the back porch.

"You know, J.D.," he said as he finished the last bite of his cookie and folded his arms on his chest, "there is room for at least ten more kids on this porch. I am going to give you an opportunity to share in this business venture of mine."

"Business venture?" I asked, not knowing what he meant. "What business venture?"

"You didn't think I let these kids see the digging of the first cesspool in Adenville for nothing, did you?" he asked as if I'd insulted him. "I charged them a penny apiece. You go round up ten more kids. Tell them they not only get to see the digging of the first cesspool for a water closet for a penny, but also that they will be served refreshments. Collect the money in advance. No credit or promises."

"How do you know Mamma will give them a cookie?" I asked.

"She has to," Tom said confidently, "because she gave all the other kids a cookie."

"What do I get out of it?" I asked. I knew from past experience that it always pays to spell out the terms when making a business deal with my brother.

"I'll pay you a commission of one penny for each five kids," Tom answered. "If you round up ten more kids, you will make two cents."

How proud I was a half hour later as I marched ten kids into our kitchen and told them to line up to receive one of Mamma's delicious oatmeal cookies. Mamma's attitude puzzled me. She didn't look pleased and proud as she had with Tom. I caught her giving me a funny look as she held the cookie jar and each kid helped himself to a cookie.

I was at the end of the line and all set to have another cookie when Mamma snapped the lid back on the jar.

"You had a cookie, John D.," she said. "Please inform Tom D. the cookie jar is empty. I wasn't prepeared to serve cookies to every boy in town."

I thought Mr. Harvey would be mad as all get out at having twenty kids watching him. But as the afternoon wore on he seemed to like playing to an audience, especially when he hit a big rock which he had to lift out of the hole. It was a heavy rock for one man to lift. All the kids applauded. Mr. Harvey looked at us and appeared to almost, but not quite, smile.

When Mr. Harvey quit work that day, he told Mamma to tell Papa that it would take two more days to finish the cesspool.

"Did you hear that, J.D.," Tom said, rubbing his hands together. "I knew my great brain would make me a fortune some day. Twenty kids tomorrow and twenty more the day after. That adds up to forty cents."

"How about me?" I asked, not wanting to be frozen out of this financial bonanza.

"I'm sorry, J.D.," he said, patting my shoulder, "but you know what Mamma said about the cookie jar. That means I'll have to buy some gingersnaps myself to serve as refreshments."

The next morning I went with Tom to Zion's Cooperative Mercantile Institution, which was the name given to stores all over Utah which were owned by the Mormon Church. There was one in every town, and you could buy anything from a penny stick of licorice to a plow and harrow in them. Most people simply called them the Z.C.M.I. store, although some Mormons did call them the Co-op. Tom bought a five-cent box of gingersnaps which contained twenty cookies.

Mr. Harvey played to a full house for the next two days. He finished digging the hole, which was over ten feet deep and about ten feet across, and a trench two feet deep and about a foot and a half wide that ran from the hole right under our house where the bathroom was located. Then he brought a wagonload of cedar posts which he used to line the sides of the cesspool, tying them together with baling wire. He also brought clay pipe, which he laid in the trench, and filled the joints with mortar. Then he covered the cesspool with cedar posts and boards over which he put two feet of dirt. He filled the trench with dirt, covering up the clay pipes just as the day's work finished.

Mamma must have felt a little guilty about not serving the kids cookies for those two days because she made lemonade for all the kids both days. Tom of course took all the credit, saying the lemonade was included in the price of admission. His great brain had made him a fortune in three days.

The failure of the new inventions Papa ordered was always made all the more embarrassing because he bragged about them in advance. The water closet was no exception. Everybody in town knew about it long before it arrived.

Nels Larson was stationmaster, ticket agent, telegrapher, express agent, and freight agent at the railroad depot. He never delivered any express or freight except the things Papa ordered. Mr. Larson would simply telephone people and tell them they had express or freight shipments at the depot and to come and get them. But his curiosity always got the best of him when anything came for Papa. When the

11

water closet arrived, he went home and got his own team and wagon to make the delivery. He told his wife the water closet had come. Mrs. Larson got right on the telephone to spread the news all over town.

By the time Mr. Larson had returned to the depot and loaded the crates containing the water closet, his wife had let everybody know that today was the day. Mr. Larson was a middle-aged man with blond hair and a light complexion stemming from his Swedish heritage. He always walked leaning forward as if walking into a strong wind and rode on the seat of his wagon the same way. He drove the team from the depot right down Main Street, with people leaving their places of business and homes to follow him. When he stopped in front of our house, there were about two hundred men, women, and children in the street. Mamma took one look out the bay window in the parlor and telephoned Papa at the *Advocate* office. Mr. Larson was poised over a wooden crate with hammer in his right hand, right in the middle of Main Street, when Papa arrived.

"What in the name of Jupiter do you think you are doing?" Papa demanded. "Make the delivery in the rear."

"Nothing in the rules, Fitz, says I've got to make deliveries in the rear," Mr. Larson said.

"You don't have to open the crates right in the middle of Main Street," Papa said.

"Rules and regulations say I've got to inspect the merchandise for damage," Mr. Larson said.

"You know very well, Nels," Papa said testily, "the only time you ever inspect anything is when the shipment is for me."

"Ain't nothing interesting in the others," Mr. Larson said.

12

"Now you listen to me, Nels," Papa said, his dark eyes flaming with anger. "I will not permit you to make a spectacle of my water closet in the middle of Main Street."

"And you listen to me, Fitz," Mr. Larson said, pointing his hammer at Papa. "It is my job to inspect the merchandise for damage and that is just what I intend to do. Don't want you blaming the railroad or the express company because this crazy contraption doesn't work."

"What makes you so certain it won't work?" Papa asked, glaring at the stationmaster.

"None of those other new-fangled inventions you ordered worked," Mr. Larson answered, putting Papa in his place.

"Go ahead and open it," Papa said in complete defeat.

The first crate Mr. Larson opened contained the copper-lined water tank, which he placed on exhibition on top of the crate. He stepped back and eyed it critically.

"Can't figure out what that is for," he said.

"Are you satisfied it isn't damaged?" Papa said as if trying to control his temper. "If so, I assure you that Mr. Harvey and I will know what it is for." Then Papa folded his arms on his chest like a martyr. "Since you are bound and determined to hold a public unveiling of my water closet in the middle of Main Street, please get on with it."

"No reason to get sore," Mr. Larson said indignantly, "just because a man is doing his job according to the rules and regulations."

The next crate contained the big brass pipe that we later learned connected the water tank near the ceiling to the bowl on the floor. Mr. Larson held it up as if it were a spyglass.

"You've been swindled again," he said to Papa as he laid the pipe down.

13

Papa was positively fuming as Mr. Larson opened the next crate which contained the porcelain bowl. Mr. Larson placed it like a trophy on top of the crate for all to see.

"It is beginning to make sense," Mr. Larson had to admit, "but that bowl is plumb too big for kids."

"Just determine if it is damaged and get on with it," Papa said, so angry he turned his back on Mr. Larson.

It wasn't until the stationmaster removed the wooden toilet seat that his skepticism began to vanish. He held it in front of his face as if it were a picture frame, as he slowly turned around for all to see.

"This is the thing-a-mah-bob you sit on!" he shouted as if making a great discovery.

There were many *ohs* and *ahs* from the crowd who were used to sitting on boards with holes cut in them.

Papa then sent me to fetch Mr. Harvey. I thought from the way Papa's jaws were puffed up that he would explode before I returned with the plumber, but he didn't. Mr. Harvey and I arrived just as the public unveiling of our water closet on Main Street came to a close.

Mr. Harvey pushed Mr. Larson to one side and began searching through the crates until he found a big brown envelope containing the instructions for assembling the water closet. Then his and Papa's troubles began. Every man, woman, and child who could get their hands on any part of the water closet as it was being carried to our bathroom thought their help entitled them to remain and watch it being assembled.

"Make everybody clear out of here," Mr. Harvey said to Papa as he plunked his tool case down on the bathroom floor. "Can't do a blooming thing with all these people hanging around in here."

Papa asked everybody to leave. Nobody budged an inch until Papa promised they could all see the water closet and how it worked after it was assembled. He even made Sweyn, Tom, and me leave.

The crowd broke up into small groups in our backyard and on our front lawn. They spoke in hushed whispers as people do at funerals. I wandered from group to group, listening. The more I listened, the more humiliated I became.

"Wouldn't want one of those things in my house," I heard Dave Teller, the shoemaker, telling a small group. "It is bound to stink up the whole house."

"Not only the house," Mr. Carter, who worked at the creamery, said, "but the whole neighborhood if that cesspool caves in during a rain storm."

My friend Howard Kay didn't help matters as he sidled up to me as if ashamed of being seen with me.

"Gosh, John," he whispered, "folks are saying your pa has gone plumb loco putting a backhouse in your bathroom." He put his fingers to his nose. "Phewee! I'd hate to be living in your house."

It was too much for me. I held back tears of humiliation until I'd run upstairs to the room I shared with Tom. I flung myself on the bed and began to cry. I had always been proud of Papa in spite of him buying crazy inventions that didn't work. But this time he'd gone too far. He had done what Aunt Bertha said he would do. He had made us Fitzgeralds the laughing stock of Adenville. Nobody would come to our house anymore. How could Mamma entertain the Ladies Sewing Circle in a house that smelled like a backhouse? It would be the same as entertaining in our old backhouse. I visualized callers at our house stopping at the front gate and putting clothespins on their noses before entering our home.

15

I don't know for how long I lay there crying with shame before I heard a terrifying clanging and banging as if somebody had dropped a lot of pans and kettles off our roof. I dropped to my knees. I was positive the water closet had exploded.

"Please, God, spare my Papa," I prayed.

Then I ran downstairs. I expected to find Mamma hysterical with grief and Papa and Mr. Harvey blown to kingdom come. Instead I found Mamma and Aunt Bertha in the kitchen making plattersful of sandwiches. I ran into the bathroom. Papa and Mr. Harvey were standing looking at the installed water closet with smug expressions on their faces. The porcelain bowl was bolted to the floor in one corner of the room that had been partitioned off. The wooden seat had been attached to it. The water tank was fastened to the wall near the ceiling, with a water pipe running up to it. The big brass pipe was connected to the water tank and the bowl. There was a brass chain attached to the water tank, with a wooden handle on it.

"One more time to make sure," Papa said to Mr. Harvey.

I watched Mr. Harvey pull on the chain. There was a clanging sound and then water rushed down the brass pipe from the water tank into the porcelain bowl, filling it up, and then suddenly the water in the bowl disappeared.

"She is ready and rarin' to go," Mr. Harvey said, and for the first time in my life I saw him smile.

It was surely a miracle invention, but there was one thing I had to know.

"Will it stink?" I asked.

"No, J.D.," Papa answered. "The water level in the bowl will keep any air or odor from coming up from the cesspool."

I was so happy that I felt like doing a jig as I followed

16

Papa to the back porch. I watched Papa clasp his hands behind his back and teeter on his heels.

"Ladies and gentlemen," Papa announced to the crowd. "I am pleased to report that Mr. Harvey and I have successfully installed the first water closet in Adenville. You will be admitted in small groups of not more than six at a time. Mr. Harvey will explain the mechanism of the water closet and how it works. He will also give each group a demonstration. As you leave please pass through the kitchen where Mrs. Fitzgerald will serve refreshments."

I was lucky that I'd seen the water closet because none of the kids got a chance to see it. Grown-ups pushed the kids aside, including Tom and Sweyn. By the time all the grown-ups had seen the water closet it was suppertime. A howl of protest went up from the kids, but their parents made them go home.

My brother Tom must have immediately put his great brain to work on how to capitalize on this because the next morning he told me to follow him to the barn.

"Run down to the Z.C.M.I. store and get me a cardboard box," he said as we entered the barn. "I'll need a piece of cardboard to make a sign."

I was curious as all get out when I returned with a cardboard box that had contained cans of condensed milk. I watched fascinated as Tom used his jacknife to cut out one side of the box. Then he laid the piece of cardboard on a bale of hay and took a package of crayons from his pocket. My admiration for his great brain turned to complete awe as I read the sign he printed on the piece of cardboard.

SEE THE MAGIC WATER CLOSET THAT DOESN'T STINK
ADMISSION ONE PENNY CASH
NO PROMISES OR CREDIT

Tom then picked up a stick, after punching two holes in the piece of cardboard. He tied the sign to the stick with twine.

"Now, J.D.," he said, "I want to hire you to be a barker and make a pitch for my new business venture."

"Barker?" I asked, not knowing what the word meant. "And what is pitch?"

"Remember last summer when Colonel Sheaffer's Medicine Show came to town?" Tom asked.

I nodded.

"Remember how Colonel Sheaffer stood on the tailgate of his medicine-show wagon, with the Indian he had with him beating on a tom-tom and the Colonel making a speech? Well, I asked the Colonel about it, and he told me that to attract a crowd you have to have a barker and make a pitch. I want you to be the barker and make a pitch to attract a crowd of kids for my new business venture."

"What is in it for me?" I asked.

"I'll give you ten per cent of the gross receipts," he answered.

"What are gross receipts?" I asked.

"All the money we take in," Tom answered. "You get one penny for every ten pennies I collect."

"It's a deal," I said gratefully.

Tom handed me the sign. Then he walked over and picked up the cowbell we put on our milk cow when we let her out to pasture. He handed the cowbell to me.

"We don't have a tom-tom like Colonel Sheaffer's Indian," he said. "Use the cowbell instead." His freckled face suddenly became solemn. "Sometimes my great brain almost scares me," he said. "I'll be a millionaire before I'm old enough to vote." Then his face broke into a grin. "Off you go, J.D. Ring the bell and make your pitch on Main Street, in front of our house."

I took up my station as barker in front of our house. I rang the cowbell and made my pitch.

"See the magic water closet that doesn't stink!" I shouted as I rang the cowbell. "Only one penny to see the magic water closet!"

Colonel Sheaffer was right. All you needed was a barker to make a pitch to attract a crowd. Kids came running from every part of town. I soon had kids lined up all the way from our front gate and around the side of the house to our back porch, where Tom was busily collecting a penny from each kid to see the water closet. My brother and I were on the verge of making a financial killing when I saw Mamma coming down Main Street. I knew she had gone to spend the morning with Mrs. Taylor who was ill. Here she was coming home and it wasn't even ten o'clock. I gave her a big smile as I rang the cowbell and made my pitch.

"See the magic water closet that doesn't stink!" I shouted. "Only one penny to see the magic water closet."

"John Dennis, come with me," Mamma said sharply.

I knew she was angry about something when she called me by my full name. She never called us boys by our full names unless she was angry with us. I followed her around the side of the house to the back porch. Tom flashed us both a triumphant grin as he collected pennies from kids before admitting them to the bathroom.

"Tom Dennis, come into the kitchen," Mamma said sternly.

One thing I loved about Mamma. When she was angry with us, she never scolded us in front of other kids. Tom and I followed her into the kitchen.

19

Aunt Bertha identified herself as the tattletale as we entered the kitchen. "I thought it best to telephone you, Tena," she said.

"And it is a good thing you did," Mamma said, placing her hands on her hips.

Calling Tom and me by our full names was bad enough, but I knew Mamma was just as angry as she could be when she placed her hands on her hips.

"Tom Dennis and John Dennis, I am thoroughly ashamed of you both," Mamma said.

"You should only be ten per cent ashamed of me," I defended myself. "I'm just the barker and only get ten per cent of the gross receipts."

"To take part in anything that is wrong even one per cent," Mamma reprimanded, "is just as bad as one hundred per cent."

Tom folded his arms on his chest. "What is wrong with using my great brain to make money?" he demanded.

"You heard your father say yesterday that everybody would be admitted to see the water closet," Mamma said. "I do not recall your father saying only adults would be admitted free and children would be charged a penny. Now, hand me those crayons in your hip pocket."

Tom reluctantly handed Mamma the box of crayons. Then Mamma took the sign away from me. I was horrified when she used a red crayon to draw a line through the words ONE PENNY and printed the word FREE instead on the sign. Then she handed the sign back to me.

"Now, John Dennis," she said to me, "let me see you put the same amount of enthusiasm into your barking, as you call it, and ringing the cowbell as you were putting into it a few minutes ago."

21

"Papa isn't going to like this one bit," Tom said. "Papa says it is brains that count and not muscles. When he finds out you made me give up a good money-making scheme my great brain thought up, he is going to be mighty angry with you, Mamma. You just wait and see."

"When your father comes home," Mamma said, not in the least cowed by Tom's threats, "I'll have him explain to you the difference between an honest business transaction and swindling your friends. And now that I think of it, you must have charged admission for letting your friends watch Mr. Harvey dig the cesspool."

"Papa didn't say anything about letting everybody watch Mr. Harvey dig the cesspool for nothing," Tom said. "And all the customers were completely satisfied."

"Your customers are going to be more than satisfied," Mamma said. "Now just march yourself out to the back porch and refund not only all the pennies you collected this morning, but also all the money you collected for letting your friends watch Mr. Harvey dig the cesspool."

"But Mamma . . ." Tom started to protest.

"You heard me, Tom Dennis," Mamma said, interrupting him.

Tom didn't have to wait until Papa came home to learn the difference between an honest business transaction and a swindle. He refunded all the pennies he'd collected for letting kids watch Mr. Harvey dig the cesspool and see the magic water closet, and there were still twenty kids in line waiting for refunds. I followed Tom into the kitchen.

"Mamma," he said indignantly, "there are a bunch of cheaters out there. I refunded all the money I collected, and do you know what, Mamma?"

"What?" Mamma asked.

"There are still twenty kids demanding refunds," Tom said with a wave of his hand toward the back porch.

"That will teach you a lesson," Mamma said as if she enjoyed seeing her own flesh and blood defrauded. "You will just have to take twenty cents out of your bank."

Tom's cheeks swelled up in protest, but he knew there was no appeal from one of Mamma's decisions. When the last kid had been paid off on the back porch, Tom put his hand on my shoulder.

"J.D. old partner," he said, "we took a twenty-cent loss on this business venture because some of those kids went back to the end of the line and got paid twice. There is no hurry making good your half of the loss, but it is always best in business to settle these things immediately. We will go get the ten cents you owe me from your bank right now, partner."

It didn't sound quite right to me. I needed some expert advice. "I'm not handing over ten cents unless Mamma tells me to," I said.

Tom put his arm around my shoulder. "We've upset Mamma enough for one day," he said. "Let us settle this like businessmen and partners should. We don't have to run to Mamma to settle a little thing like this."

I guess I would have handed over my ten cents of the loss if Mamma hadn't been in the kitchen when we entered it to go upstairs to our room and get the money. I explained the whole deal to Mamma and asked her to settle it.

"John D. was only a ten per cent partner," Mamma said, to my joy. "He is therefore only responsible for ten per cent of the loss."

Tom didn't take the decision lying down. "But you said anything that was one per cent wrong was just the same as one hundred per cent. That makes J.D. a full partner."

Mamma wasn't swayed by Tom's brilliant defense. "I was speaking of morals," she said. "Morally John D. is as guilty as you. But looking at it from a business angle, you would have pocketed ninety per cent of the profits if Aunt Bertha hadn't phoned me. That makes you responsible for ninety per cent of the loss."

Tom knew the decision was final. "All right, J.D.," he said, "I'll settle for two cents."

"Just one moment, boys," Mamma said. "John D. gave you back the two cents commission you paid him. He wasn't your partner when Mr. Harvey was digging the cesspool. He was working for you on a straight commission. That makes you two even."

It was the first time that my brother's great brain had cost him money. I was positive Tom would carry the scar of this financial catastrophe to his grave.

CHAPTER TWO

Revenge Can Be Sour

MISS THATCHER, WHO HAD been ill with a very bad cold, was well enough to start teaching again on the following Monday. If she had been younger, she might have recovered sooner, but Miss Thatcher was getting along in years and we kids had heard talk that she might be replaced in the fall. Sweyn, Tom, and I were back in school just one week when school stopped again for all of us because of Mamma's system with childhood diseases. Sweyn, being the oldest, usually caught a childhood disease first. Tom caught the diseases Sweyn missed. And that made me the victim of Mamma's system every time because Mamma believed in getting us all infected with a disease at the same time and getting it over with.

I had a feeling Friday evening during supper that I was about to become the victim again.

Mamma looked across the table at Sweyn. "Do your eyes hurt, Sweyn D.?" she asked.

"A little," Sweyn admitted.

The next morning Mamma took one look at Sweyn and ordered him to get undressed and go to her bedroom on the ground floor. Whenever we boys were sick, she always put us in her bedroom. That was the first part of her system. Then she telephoned Dr. LeRoy.

Mamma's bedroom had a door that adjoined the bathroom. When the doctor arrived, Tom and I sneaked into the bathroom. Tom's great brain had long ago figured out a way to eavesdrop. He put a water glass against the door leading to Mamma's bedroom and to his ear. I watched his face as he listened. I knew the news was going to be bad as the expression on his face changed from curiosity to dejection.

"S.D. has got the measles," he said sadly as he stepped back from the door. "You know what that means, J.D."

"Maybe we can sneak out and play before Mamma puts us to bed," I suggested.

Mamma must have guessed what I had in my mind because she opened the door leading to her bedroom. She caught Tom red-handed with the water glass in his hand.

"I suspected as much," she said. "You boys know what to do."

Tom shook his head slowly. "It seems silly for J.D. and me to get the measles just because Sweyn got them," he said. "Maybe J.D. and I are immune to the measles."

"If you are immune," Mamma said, "we will soon find out."

"But Mamma," I protested, "I never get a chance to

catch a disease first. Sweyn will be all well just when Tom and I are getting sick. And when Tom catches a disease first, he is all well just when Sweyn and I are getting sick. It ain't fair, Mamma."

"Isn't fair," Mamma said. "I don't want to hear another word."

There was nothing to do but obey. Tom and I went upstairs to the bedroom we shared. We undressed and put on our nightshirts and bathrobes. We dutifully marched down to Mamma's bedroom. Mamma and Aunt Bertha had hung blankets over the windows to make the room dark. The room had to be dark when you had the measles because the light hurt your eyes. Tom and I groped our way to bed and crawled in with Sweyn. We had to stay in bed with Sweyn until we were both good and infected with measles.

Later when Dr. LeRoy came to the house and pronounced Tom and me good and infected by Sweyn, Mamma let us move back up to our bedroom.

Sure enough, just like always, as Sweyn was getting better Tom and I started getting watery eyes, runny noses, and fevers. Sweyn moved upstairs to his bedroom while Tom and I moved down to Mamma's bedroom.

The next morning Sweyn came into Mamma's bedroom right after breakfast to rub salt in our wounds as he always did when he got a disease first.

"Good morning," he said so cheerfully I would have thrown a pillow at him if I could have seen him in the darkened room. "How are all my little measle patients today?" he asked.

"Beat it," Tom said.

"I was just about to do that very thing," Sweyn said.

28

"While you two are lying here moaning and groaning with pain, I will be outside playing and having fun."

"You can't do that," Tom said. "We are quarantined."

"True," Swyn admitted, "but it so happens my good friend Jerry Mason has had the German measles and Dr. LeRoy and Mamma said he could come here to play."

"Why don't you really rub it in and tell J.D. you'll celebrate his birthday for him?" Tom asked with sarcasm.

"That's right," Sweyn said as if the idea pleased him. "Can you imagine J.D. celebrating his birthday in bed with the measles? What a way to spend a birthday."

I was so sick I'd forgotten about my birthday. Spending my birthday in bed with the measles wasn't bothering me because I knew Mamma would give me a delayed birthday party when I was well. What was bothering me was knowing I would never be the first to catch a disease. I would never be the one to be all well just as Tom and Sweyn were getting sick. I would never know the joy of coming into Mamma's bedroom and rubbing salt in their wounds the way they did to me.

Every day Sweyn came into the bedroom to tell us about all the good things he'd had to eat that day while Tom and I had to eat just mush and soup. Every day Sweyn rubbed it in by telling us what he and Jerry Mason planned to do that day while we lay sick in bed.

Tom and I finally got over the measles. The quarantine sign on our house came down and we three boys went back to school.

Mamma gave me a delayed birthday party on a Saturday afternoon. All my friends came to the party. We played Heavy Heavy Hangs Over My Poor Head, Button Button

Who Has the Button, Hide the Thimble, Pin the Tail on the Donkey, and other wonderful games.

All my friends gave me presents, but the best present of all was the genuine Indian beaded belt my Uncle Mark gave me. Uncle Mark was the town marshal and a deputy sheriff. He was married to Papa's sister, my Aunt Cathie. Tom was bug-eyed when he saw the belt. He tried to trade me out of it and then he tried to swindle me out of it, but I was too smart for him. I was the only kid in town with a genuine Indian beaded belt and I wasn't about to let go of it for anything.

On Wednesday of the following week I missed my friend Howard Kay at school. Sweyn, Tom, and I had been staying after school every afternoon to make up for the days we'd lost. When Miss Thatcher finally let us go, I ran all the way to the Kay home. There was a yellow quarantine sign on the house. I knew from the color of the sign that Howard must have the mumps. Wasn't this just my luck. Why couldn't Howard have had his mumps while I was having the measles.

That night as Tom and I undressed for bed I hung my Indian belt on the bedstead.

"It's a beauty," Tom said, eyeing the belt. "There must be something you want more than the belt, J.D."

"Nothing you've got," I said, thinking about Howard and his mumps.

"Then there is something!" Tom said eagerly. "Just name it, J.D., and we can make a deal."

"The mumps," I said. "Only I've got to get them first."

"You must be crazy," Tom said. "I could tell you how to get the mumps first, but knowing Mamma's system I'd have to get them too. The belt isn't worth it."

I lay awake putting my little brain to work. If Tom

knew how I could get the mumps first, there must be a way. I thought and I thought and I thought about it. When Sweyn or Tom got a disease, Mamma made sure I caught it by putting me into bed with them. That was why they quarantined people who had contagious diseases—so they couldn't give the disease to anybody else. Now, if there was just some way for me to sneak into Howard Kay's house and get him to infect me with the mumps, I'd have the last laugh on Tom and Sweyn. My little brain had done it! I felt like jumping out of bed and dancing round the room.

I found that sneaking into Howard's house wasn't going to be easy. I decided it would have to be on a Saturday because there just wasn't time after school with Miss Thatcher keeping me and my brothers in to make up work we'd lost.

Saturday morning after filling up the woodboxes and coal buckets in the kitchen and parlor and helping Tom and Sweyn feed and water the chickens, our team of horses, the milk cow, and Sweyn's mustang pony, I climbed to the top of our barn. I could see over the Olsens' backyard. I could also see the back porch of Howard's house. I thought Mrs. Kay would never come out of her house, but she finally did. She had on a big sunbonnet and carried some packages of seeds in her hands. She headed straight for her vegetable garden.

I climbed down from the barn. I walked boldly down Main Street, past the Kay home, and around to an alley. I cut through the Smiths' orchard, pretending I was taking a shortcut. In the middle of the orchard I dropped to my knees. I kept out of sight on my hands and knees until I'd crawled to the Smiths' backyard. I couldn't see anybody on the Smiths' back porch. I crawled along a hedge separating the Smiths' place from the Kays' place. If anybody saw me, I could pretend I'd come over to play with Seth Smith. But nobody saw me. I came to an opening in the hedge, which Howard, Seth, and I used when playing Indian scout. I squeezed through the opening and ran to the side porch of the Kay house.

I went upstairs to Howard's room. It was empty. I peeked out the upstairs window. Mrs. Kay was bent over her vegetable garden, planting seeds. I went downstairs where I knew there were two bedrooms. I heard Howard coughing in his mother's bedroom. I almost burst out laughing when I opened the door and saw Howard. His cheeks and jaws were all puffed up like a balloon with a funny face painted on it.

"You can't come in here," Howard whispered.

I walked over to the bed. I bent over and put my face close to his face. "Breathe on me and infect me with the mumps," I said.

"Have you gone loco?" he asked. "The mumps hurt like the devil. It even hurts to talk."

"If you are a true pal, you'll infect me with the mumps," I pleaded. "It is the only way I can get even with Tom and Sweyn. One of them always gets a disease first. That means they are all over it just when I'm getting sick. I want to be the first one to get well just once, so I can rub it in good the way they do to me."

"All right," Howard said, "but I still think you are loco wanting to catch the mumps."

Howard proved to be a true pal. He put his face close to mine and breathed into it as I inhaled. We were going just great, with me getting infected, when we heard the screen door on the back porch slam.

"Now we are in for it," Howard whispered as he looked wildly around the room. "Quick! Hide under the bed."

I dived under the bed just in time. I could see Mrs. Kay's shoes and ankles as she came into the room.

"Are you all right, dear?" she asked.

"I'm fine, Mom," Howard answered.

"I just want to finish planting the radishes," his mother said. "I won't be long."

Mrs. Kay left the room. I crawled out from under the bed. I sat down on the edge of the bed and put my face close to Howard's. He breathed into my face, with me inhaling, until we decided I was good and infected.

"You are a real pal," I said.

"If you say so, John," Howard said as if he doubted it.

I couldn't help feeling proud of myself as I made my way home the same way I'd come. This was one time when I would surely get a disease first. And just when I was getting over the mumps, Tom and Sweyn would be coming down with them. I could picture my brothers lying in bed, with their cheeks and jaws all swollen, and suffering after I was all better. Boy, was I going to get even!

I looked in the mirror every morning to see if there was any swelling in my jaws. Nothing happened. I had never felt so let down in my life. With the coming of Friday morning and still no sign of the mumps, I came to the conclusion that I hadn't been infected enough. The next morning I did my chores in jig time and climbed on top of the barn. I could see Mrs. Kay leaning over the backyard fence, talking to Mrs. Smith next door. Mamma had once said that Mrs. Smith could out-talk any four women in town. If Mamma was right, and I'd never known her to be wrong, Mrs. Kay would be there a long time.

I climbed down from the roof of the barn and ran all the way to the Smith home. I boldly walked into the front yard, hoping Seth wasn't home. If he was, I'd just pretend I came over to play with him. Luck was with me. I made my way to the hole in the hedge without anybody seeing me. In another minute I was in the bedroom with Howard.

"Gosh, John, what are you doing here?" he exclaimed.

"I didn't catch them," I said. "Maybe you didn't infect me enough."

"It ain't time yet," Howard said. "Dr. LeRoy said it takes from twelve days to three weeks after being exposed."

"Exposed?" I asked, wondering if I'd missed something.

"It's the same as infected," Howard explained.

"As long as I am here," I said, "we might as well make sure that I'm exposed plenty."

Howard obliged like a true pal. He even suggested it might be a good idea to cough in my face a few times, although it hurt him like the devil to cough. Never did a boy have such a true friend. Howard breathed in my face and coughed in my face until we were positive I was exposed for sure.

I was the saddest kid in town when fourteen days had passed since my first visit to Howard without me coming down with the mumps. A horrible thought came to me. Maybe I was one of those unfortunate kids who was immune to the mumps. I decided to find out by asking Mamma to look at my throat. She was in the kitchen with Aunt Bertha. They were making pies.

"Mamma, will you look at my throat?" I asked.

She wiped flour from her hands onto her apron. There was concern in her hazel eyes as she placed a hand on my forehead.

"Don't you feel well, John D.?" she asked.

"That's the trouble," I said with disgust. "I feel fine."

"Then why do you want me to look at your throat?" she asked.

I almost tipped the beans but caught myself in time. "It tickles," I said.

Mamma looked at my throat. She assured me there was nothing the matter with it. Little did she know her cruel words were breaking my heart.

Three days later when I got up to get washed and dressed and have breakfast before going to school, my throat really did tickle and feel sore. I didn't pay any attention to it because I was now convinced I was immune to the mumps.

During supper that evening Mamma kept looking at me across the table. "Does it hurt you to chew, John D.?" she asked.

"It hurts my jaws a little," I answered. Then it hit me what this meant.

"Let me have a look at you," Mamma said.

I got up and walked around the table, feeling ten feet tall. Maybe I wasn't immune to the mumps after all.

Mamma pressed her fingers to my throat. "Does that hurt?" she asked.

"It hurts," I said happily. I had never known what joy there was to pain until that moment.

"There seems to be some swelling," Mamma said.

"Are you sure, Mamma?" I asked gleefully as I flashed Sweyn and Tom a triumphant grin.

"I don't know why it pleases you so," Mamma said. "I think you are coming down with the mumps. Finish eating your supper and go to bed. I'll have Dr. LeRoy come by to have a look at you."

"Hurray!" I couldn't help shouting as I did a little jig around the table back to my place.

Papa stared at me. "Better get him to bed immediately," he said to Mamma. "The boy has such a fever he doesn't know what he is doing."

I was all undressed and in bed in the upstairs bedroom I shared with Tom when Dr. LeRoy came into the room followed by Mamma. He pressed his fingers against my throat. He made me open my mouth while he looked at my throat. He took my temperature.

"It's the mumps all right," he said to Mamma.

Never in my life had I heard such wonderful news. I had a hard time staying in bed until they left the room. Then I got up and was doing a happy jig when Sweyn and Tom entered.

Sweyn grabbed me and threw me onto the bed. "Papa was right," he said to Tom. "Old J.D. has gone crazy with the fever."

"Ha! Ha! Ha!" I laughed, although it hurt my jaws to laugh. "I got them first."

"Let him go," Tom said to Sweyn. "J.D. hasn't got a fever. He got the mumps on purpose."

Sweyn let me go and stood up. "Then he *must* be crazy," he said.

"Crazy like a fox," I said, sitting on the edge of the bed and grinning triumphantly at my brothers. "Maybe I've only got a little brain, but I figured out how to get a disease first for a change. I sneaked into Howard Kay's house while he had the mumps and got him to expose me."

Sweyn was so angry that he grabbed my shoulders and began shaking me. "Mean to tell me you deliberately got the mumps just so you could give them to me and T.D.?"

"You guessed it," I said and couldn't help gloating. "It will take two to three weeks under Mamma's system for you

36

and T.D. to get them. By that time I will be all well. I'll be the one who rubs it in. I'll be the one who is out playing while you two are lying in bed, groaning with pain."

I didn't mind telling them because I knew my brothers were not tattletales. They made no protest when Mamma moved me down to her bedroom and made both of them get into bed with me to get infected. They did torture me when the mumps got so bad I could only swallow mush and soup. They would come into the room, chewing on a drumstick or eating a piece of cake or pie, and smack their lips as they told me how good it tasted. They spent a fortune on candy just to eat it in front of me, knowing with the mumps I couldn't take a bite of candy because of the pain in chewing. Finally I could stand it no longer. I protested against this barbaric torture to Mamma.

"I think your brothers have every right to tease you this way," Mamma said.

"Tease me!" I cried out. "It is worse than Indian torture."

"Then bear it like an Indian," Mamma said. "I was a bit suspicious when you seemed so happy to get the mumps. I put two and two together and had a talk with Mrs. Kay. She in turn had a talk with her son Howard. I think you deserve the punishment your brothers are giving you."

I was positive I would starve to death or go out of my mind as Sweyn and Tom continued to torture me. But I made it. My day of glory finally arrived. I was all well while Tom and Sweyn lay groaning with pain in Mamma's bedroom, with their cheeks and jaws swelled up like they had two baseballs in their mouths.

Mamma made fresh bread that day. If there was anything my two brothers liked the most, it was to take the heel of a fresh-baked loaf of bread, smother it with butter and sugar, and then put it in the oven until the sugar turned brown. It was better than candy. I entered the bedroom with a heel of bread covered with butter and toasted sugar.

"I thought I'd have a little snack before going out to play," I said as I waved the heel of bread back and forth so they could smell it. Then I took a bite out of it. "Boy is this delicious. Don't you wish you could have a bite?"

They were so jealous neither one of them said anything as I ate the heel, and they watched me with their mouths watering. Then I pulled out a stick of red licorice. I took a bite out of it.

"I'd offer you fellows a bite but I know you can't chew anything," I said. "I guess I'll have to eat it all by myself." And then I really rubbed it in. "I'll be thinking of you fellows during supper tonight," I said. "Mamma is having fried chicken and I know how you both love fried chicken. And while you are having only soup to eat, I'll be stuffing myself with good old fried chicken and a piece of Aunt Bertha's delicious apple pie."

"Beat it," Sweyn said, unable to endure the torture any longer.

"As soon as I finish my licorice," I said, taking another bite of it. "Then I'm going outside to play. You'll hear me whistling and shouting happily as I play outside the bedroom window so you can hear, while you two lie here groaning and moaning."

Tom suddenly sat up in bed. "I've got news for you, J.D.," he said, making a face because it hurt his throat to talk. "Beginning right now, S.D. and I are going to give you the silent treatment. And because of the dirty trick you played on us, we are going to give you the silent treatment

for a whole month after we are well." He looked at Sweyn who nodded. "These are the last words you'll hear from me or S.D. until a month after we are well."

The silent treatment! I hadn't thought about that. Papa and Mamma had a system for punishing us boys when we did something wrong. They never gave us a whipping like other kids got from their parents. When they wanted to punish us, they both just stopped speaking to us. Sometimes the silent treatment lasted only one day. Sometimes it would last a whole week. It was ten times worse than getting a whipping. They would both pretend we didn't even exist. Even while eating, if I asked Mamma or Papa to pass the butter, they would pretend they didn't hear me, and Tom or Sweyn or Aunt Bertha would have to pass it to me.

I soon discovered that the silent treatment by Papa and Mamma was mild compared to the silent treatment by Tom and Sweyn. They took all the joy out of me being able to rub it in about them being sick and me being well. When I went into the bedroom, they both just turned over on their stomachs and ignored me. I also discovered there was no joy in being able to play without Tom. It was as if I'd lost the one thing that made playing fun. My revenge had turned sour. My life was lonely and miserable during the days Tom and Sweyn were confined to bed with the mumps. I cried myself to sleep at night after praying to God to never let my little brain get any more foolish ideas.

Little did I know the worst was yet to come. When Tom and Sweyn were well enough to be up and around, they both continued to give me the silent treatment. Tom refused to speak to me or play with me and so did Sweyn. I went through three days of torture before Tom relented one night as we undressed for bed.

40

"That was a dirty trick you pulled on S.D. and me," he said as he pulled off his pants. "Do you admit it was a dirty trick?"

"Yes," I answered. Just having him speak to me even this way made me feel better.

"And do you admit you should be punished for it?" Tom asked.

"Yes, but not too much punishment," I cried. "I'll go crazy if you and S.D. give me the silent treatment for a whole month."

"There are two ways to punish you," Tom said as he folded his pants and put them on a chair. "Giving you the silent treatment for a month is one."

"I'll die if you do," I said. Then I took hope. "You said there were two ways. What is the other way?"

"The other way would be to make you give up something you want to keep," he said. "If you agreed to give up something you really like, I would get S.D. to call off the silent treatment with me."

"I'll give you anything I've got," I said happily.

"Even the Indian beaded belt Uncle Mark gave you for your birthday?" Tom asked.

The belt was the envy of every kid in town. It was a stiff price to pay. I hesitated.

"Forget it, J.D.," Tom said. "These are the last words I'll speak to you for a whole month."

I hesitated no longer. "You can have the belt," I said quickly before he might change his mind.

Tom got up from the bed where he was sitting. I watched him walk to my chair, remove the belt from my pants, and hang it on his chair.

"And to show you my heart is in the right place," he

41

said, "I'm not going to charge you anything for getting Sweyn to lift the silent treatment."

I threw my arms around him and hugged him. "You sure are good to me," I said gratefully.

"That is what brothers are for," Tom said. "Good-night, J.D."

It was worth the belt just to have him talk to me and say good-night to me. Before going to sleep that night, I included Tom in my prayers and thanked God for giving me such a big-hearted and wonderful brother.

CHAPTER THREE

The Great Brain Saves the Day

WITH THE END OF THE silent treatment, I could look forward to three big events. School was over for the year. Tom and Sweyn had promised to teach me how to swim. And I was going to mate my dog, Brownie, with a dog named Lady. Brownie was the only dog we had ever owned who wasn't a mongrel. He was a purebred Alaskan. A rancher who was a friend of Papa's had given me the pup on my fifth birthday.

I guess because Brownie was a thoroughbred, it made him different. He didn't run and play with other dogs, but he would fight them if they wanted to fight. He was such a good fighter that it wasn't long until every dog in town was afraid of him. If any dog came near him, Brownie would show his teeth and begin to growl and chase them away.

Every kid in town who owned a female dog wanted to mate it with Brownie. But my dog wanted nothing to do with them. It sure looked as if Brownie would never be a father, until the Jensen brothers got a sheep dog named Lady from their uncle. Lady was the first dog that Brownie didn't chase away when she came near him. To my surprise he even ran and played with her.

I knew Tom had this on his mind when he approached me with a proposition. We were sitting on our back porch steps just sort of lazily enjoying the beginning of the summer vacation.

"J.D.," Tom said, "let me arrange to mate Brownie with Lady and I'll see to it you get the pick of the litter of pups."

"I don't need you to arrange it," I said, thinking he was going to charge me for it. "As the owner of the male dog I get the pick of the litter anyway."

"You will probably pick the worst pup in the litter," he said.

He had me there. All puppies looked alike to me.

"How much is it going to cost me?" I asked cautiously.

"How can you think such a thing?" Tom asked indignantly. "You know I'm very sharp when it comes to judging puppies. I just don't want my own brother to get stung."

"You mean you'll do it for nothing?" I asked, unable to believe my ears.

"Of course, J.D.," he said. "But we'll have to wait until Lady is in heat."

"What's heat?" I asked.

"A female dog can have pups twice a year," Tom said. "And that time of the year is when she is in heat."

"How do you know when it happens?" I asked.

"For one thing the female dog will start acting kind of silly every time it sees a male dog," he answered. "And when in heat, the female dog gives off a peculiar odor. When the male dog smells this odor, he knows the female dog wants to mate."

"It's a deal," I said. "And remember, you said there would be no charge."

A few days later during breakfast Tom and Sweyn told Papa they were going to take me down to the river and teach me how to swim that afternoon. I was so excited that I thought the morning would never end. And then after lunch we had to wait an hour before we could go swimming, knowing if we went any sooner we might get cramps.

We ran into Frank and Allan Jensen on our way to the river. They had Lady with them. Frank was Tom's age and his brother was the same age as Sweyn. They were blond kids with hair that was almost white. Shocks of it protruded from beneath their caps like bangs over their foreheads.

"Lady is in heat now," Allan said. "How about bringing Brownie over to our place tomorrow and we'll put them in our barn?"

"We'll be there," Tom said.

"You fellows going swimming?" Sweyn asked.

"No," Allan said. "We are going exploring. Want to come along?"

"We can't today," Tom said. "We promised to teach J.D. how to swim."

We left the Jensen brothers and Lady and continued on to the swimming hole in the river. We stripped naked. There were about a dozen kids already swimming and diving as I followed Tom and Sweyn to the bank of the river. Sweyn then led me into the river until the water was up to my armpits.

"I'm going to hold your chin, J.D.," he said. "You paddle dog-fashion and kick your legs."

I was scared but felt safe as long as Sweyn was holding my chin as he took me into deeper water.

"Now keep paddling and kicking," Sweyn said as he let go of my chin.

My head went under water. I tried to scream only to swallow more water. I was sure I was going to drown and let everybody know it as my head came above the water. Sweyn grabbed hold of my hair and pulled me into shallow water. He and Tom looked completely disgusted as they led me out of the river.

Tom looked at Sweyn. "Well?" he asked.

"I guess it is the only way," Sweyn said.

My oldest brother grabbed me and picked me up in his arms. I screamed bloody murder and tried to wiggle loose. He held me tight as he carried me up the plank used as a diving board over the deepest part of the swimming hole. I knew this was how almost every kid in town learned to swim, but I wanted no part of it.

"Let me go!" I screamed. "I'll drown for sure."

"You won't drown," Sweyn said. "You just keep paddling dog-fashion with your hands and kicking your legs and you won't drown. And it won't do you any good to yell for help, J.D., because I'm not going to jump in after you."

"Please let me go," I begged, more afraid than I'd ever been in my life.

"Stop that blubbering," Sweyn ordered me, "or I'll tell Papa you acted like a coward and disgraced the name of Fitzgerald before all these kids."

46

I stopped bawling. Sweyn had given me no other choice. I might as well drown as have him tell Papa I was a coward.

"Here you go, J.D.," Sweyn yelled as he tossed me from the diving board into the deepest part of the swimming hole. He sounded as if he enjoyed drowning his own brother.

I hit the water and went down until my feet touched bottom. I tried to scream and got a bellyful of water. I began paddling with my hands and kicking my legs like sixty. Then my head came out of the water. I breathed in air.

"Atta boy!" I heard Tom yell.

I was too interested in saving my own life to pay any attention to him. I was sure I was going to drown before I reached the bank of the river. Then my fingers touched mud. I never knew mud could feel so good as I crawled up the river bank.

Sweyn and Tom patted me on the back.

"You swam more than twenty feet," Sweyn said.

Tom nodded. "But next time don't scream and yell," he said. "Keep your mouth shut."

"The next time?" I asked, and felt myself get sick inside.

"As soon as you get your wind," Tom said.

"Right," Sweyn said. "And this time you are going to run and jump off the diving board all by yourself."

"I am not," I said as I started for my clothes. "I'm going home."

Sweyn grabbed me. "You run and jump off that diving board or I'll keep throwing you off it until you do."

"And we'll let the kids chaw-raw-beef your clothes," Tom threatened.

I don't know if I was more frightened of jumping off the diving board or having my clothes chaw-raw-beefed. A kid had to be disliked a lot to have his clothes chaw-raw-

47

beefed, which consisted of soaking them in the river and then tying the socks, shirt, pants, and underwear in tight knots.

"Papa and Mamma will never forgive you two if I drown," I said, feeling like a martyr.

"And," Tom said, "they will never forgive you if you turn out to be a coward."

I knew there was no way out. Every kid at the swimming hole was watching as I started for the diving board. My legs trembled so much I could hardly walk. I was only eight years old and going to my death. I stopped as I reached the diving board. I looked down the river. All I had to do was to run down the river bank and into the bushes. But if I did, I could never go home again. I was pretty young to go into the mountains and live like a naked savage. If I ran now, I would be a coward. Better by far to drown than to disgrace our family name.

I took a deep breath and ran right up the diving board and jumped into the swimming hole. This time I held my breath and kept my mouth shut as I paddled and kicked my way to the surface. Then I began paddling furiously with my arms and kicking my legs. The next thing I knew I had reached the river bank. All the kids ran up to congratulate me. It was the proudest moment of my life. I wasn't afraid of the water anymore. As soon as I got my wind I ran and jumped off the diving board again.

I was waiting on the front porch with Tom and Sweyn when Papa came home from the *Adenville Weekly Advocate* office that evening.

"Well, J.D.," Papa said, smiling at me, "did you learn how to swim today?"

48

"Yes, Papa," I said, and had to restrain myself not to brag about it.

"He's a regular duck," Sweyn said. "He ran and jumped off the diving board and swam to the river bank a dozen times."

Papa took out his purse and removed a quarter. "I think you deserve a reward, J.D., for learning how to swim in one day." He handed me the quarter.

As soon as Papa entered the house Tom looked at me. "Why should Papa give you a quarter when it was S.D. and I who taught you how to swim? Of course, J.D., if you want to be greedy and keep it all for yourself, I guess that is your business."

I was feeling so proud of myself I would have gladly shared the quarter with my brothers on the spot if Sweyn hadn't come to my rescue.

"For gosh sakes, T.D.," he said as if disgusted with Tom, "can't you let anybody have a nickel to themselves without trying to connive them out of it?" Then he looked at me. "Go put the money in your bank, J.D., before The Great Brain figures out a way to take it away from you."

We were eating supper that evening when the telephone rang with one long ring and two short rings.

"That is for us," Mamma said as she got up from the table.

Mamma went into the hallway to answer the phone. When she returned, she looked worried.

"That was Mrs. Jensen," she said as she sat down at the table. "Did you boys see Frank or Allan today?"

Tom nodded. "We met them on our way to the swimming hole this afternoon.

49

"Did they go swimming with you?" Mamma asked.

"No," Tom answered. "They said they were going exploring."

"What is the matter, Tena?" Papa asked.

"They didn't come home for supper," Mamma answered.

"The boys probably didn't realize how late it was getting," Papa said.

"Just the same," Mamma said, "I am going over there as soon as we finish eating. You boys help Bertha with the dishes."

Papa didn't appear worried until it was almost our bedtime, when Uncle Mark stopped by. Uncle Mark came into the parlor. The light from the chandelier was shining on the marshal's badge pinned to his shirt.

"I am going to organize a posse to search for the Jensen boys," he told Papa with a worried look on his deeply tanned face.

Tom laid aside *The World Almanac* which he had been reading. "I can give you a clue, Uncle Mark," he said. "Allan had a candle sticking out of his hip pocket when we met him and Frank this afternoon. They told us they were going exploring."

"I was afraid of that," Uncle Mark said. "The boys were last seen near Skeleton Cave."

I couldn't blame Uncle Mark for being worried. The first thing every kid in Adenville had to promise when he went exploring was not to go near Skeleton Cave. It was a mammoth cave that had never been explored. Papa had told us the cave apparently had several levels, with passages and labyrinths extending for miles. The only part of the cave that had been explored was the big entrance chamber and a passageway leading to a smaller chamber. In the smaller chamber there were fantastic limestone and stalactite formations. Passages led off from the smaller chamber in two directions. It was called Skeleton Cave because two skeletons had been found inside the smaller chamber.

Papa put on his hat and coat and left with Uncle Mark. Mamma came home a few minutes later. She made us boys go straight to bed. I was so frightened I didn't think I could fall asleep. When I did, I had a nightmare about Tom and me being lost in the cave.

When Tom, Sweyn, and I entered the kitchen for breakfast the next morning, I could tell from Mamma's eyes that she had been crying. Papa looked as if he had been up all night.

"Did they find them?" Sweyn asked as we sat down at the big kitchen table.

Papa shook his head as he helped himself to some fried eggs and bacon from the big platter on the table. "There isn't any doubt the boys are lost in the cave," he said.

Tom, Sweyn, and I ate as fast as Mamma would let us. Then she made us remain at the table until Papa was through eating. We ran all the way to Cedar Ridge where the entrance to Skeleton Cave was located. It looked as if the whole population of Adenville was on Cedar Ridge, standing around in large and small groups. We arrived just as Uncle Mark drove up with Mr. Harmon of the Z.C.M.I. store sitting beside him on the wagon seat. I could see six big bales of half-inch rope and a dozen lanterns in the wagon. Uncle Mark drove the team right up to the entrance to Skeleton Cave.

"What are they going to do?" I asked with a feeling of awe.

"The rope is so the search party can find their way back

out of the cave," Tom explained. "And they will need the lanterns for light. Let's go someplace where we can see into the big chamber of the cave."

Sweyn and I followed Tom to a big boulder. Sweyn boosted me and Tom up first. Then Tom lay on his belly with me sitting on his legs to hold him while he helped Sweyn up. From the top of the boulder we could see right into the big entrance chamber of the cave.

Uncle Mark, Mr. Harmon, Mr. Jensen, and half a dozen other men quickly unloaded the wagon. Then Uncle Mark took one end of a bale of rope and tied it securely to a big boulder in the entrance chamber. Then with several men helping him Uncle Mark began unwinding the bale of rope and coiling the rope carefully. When they finished with the first bale, Uncle Mark tied the end of it to the beginning of the next bale, and they began unwinding that bale with Uncle Mark coiling the rope carefully. They kept doing this until all six bales of rope had been spliced together and they had one continuous piece of rope.

"Those are five-hundred-foot bales of rope," Tom said. "That means the searching party can enter into the cave for a distance of three thousand feet."

We watched as Uncle Mark took one end of the spliced rope and tied it around his waist. Then he picked up a lantern and lighted it. We saw him motion to Mr. Jensen and several other men to pick up lanterns and light them. Then with Uncle Mark in the lead and with Mr. Jensen and five other men each carrying a lighted lantern and holding on to the rope, they all disappeared into the passageway leading to the smaller chamber in the cave.

I lay on my stomach on the big boulder and watched with a feeling of horror as the spliced coil of rope began to

the one continuous piece of rope made a large pile in the big chamber of the cave.

"With those eight bales," Tom said, "added to the other six bales, the search party can now penetrate a distance of seven thousand feet into the cave. That is more than a mile."

"We aren't going to be able to watch it," Sweyn said. "By the time we get home and do our chores it will be time for supper."

Mamma made us go to bed at our usual time that night despite our protests. The next morning at breakfast we learned from Papa that Frank and Allan and Lady hadn't been found, although the search had gone on all through the night. We had just finished eating when Uncle Mark came to the house. He had a two-day growth of beard on his face and had been without sleep for two nights.

"I'd like to see you alone," he said to Papa.

They went into the parlor with Papa shutting the sliding doors between the dining room and parlor.

I followed Tom out to our backyard because I knew what he was going to do. His great brain had long ago figured out a way to eavesdrop on anybody in our parlor. We were without doubt the best-informed kids in town on things parents didn't want their children to hear.

I watched Tom climb up to the roof of our back porch and then crawl up the edge of the roof until he was on top of the house. I held my breath as he stood up like a tightrope walker and walked across the pointed top of the roof until he came to the chimney for the fireplace in our parlor. He got hold of the top of the stone chimney and, using a crack for a footrest, hoisted himself up until his head was above the chimney. My brother had told me the stone chimney of the fireplace magnified voices in our parlor so he could hear every word spoken.

I waited nervously for Tom, who seemed to be taking his time listening. At last I saw him coming back down. His freckled face was grim as he jumped down from the roof of our back porch and joined me.

"Uncle Mark doesn't seem to think they will ever find Frank and Allan and Lady," he told me.

"Is he going to give up?" I asked, shivering as I thought of poor Frank and Allan and Lady doomed to die in the blackness of Skeleton Cave.

"They're going to keep trying," Tom said, "but Uncle Mark says it is hopeless. He told Papa the search party found an underground river in the cave, and Frank and Allan and Lady could have fallen into it and drowned. He said that the current is so swift it could have carried them all to their deaths."

"Gosh, T.D.," I said sadly, "that means Frank and Allan and Lady are gonners for sure."

"Even if they are alive," Tom said, "Uncle Mark told Papa they are probably going farther and farther into the cave, trying to find their way out. And he said it would take an army months to fully explore all levels of the cave." Tom shook his head. "If they don't find them alive it is going to cost me a fortune."

"How do you mean it will cost you a fortune?" I asked.

"Skip it, J.D.," Tom said quickly, too quickly.

"Maybe your great brain can save the day," I said without much hope.

Tom straightened up. "Now that the grown-ups have just about given up," he said, "I guess it is up to me to save

56

Frank, Allan, and Lady. I'll put my great brain to work on it."

We walked to our barn. Tom gave me orders to stand guard and not let anybody in the barn. Then he went into the barn and climbed the rope ladder up to his loft to put his great brain to work.

I was disappointed when Mamma called us for lunch. Tom came down from his loft when I hollered up to him. He reported that his great brain hadn't came up with a plan for saving Frank, Allan, and Lady.

"But don't worry, J.D.," he said confidently. "My great brain has never failed me."

After we had eaten lunch, Tom went back up to his loft while I stood guard outside the barn. Brownie came into the corral. He wanted to play. I always played and romped and wrestled with Brownie because he never played with other dogs before Lady had come along. He began barking as we started to play. I was afraid the barking would disturb Tom and tried to make Brownie stop. He thought this was more playing and barked louder. The barn door suddenly opened and Tom came out. I thought he was going to be mad at me for letting Brownie bark. Instead he flashed me a triumphant grin.

"I knew my great brain would save the day," he said. "Come with me, J.D., and bring Brownie with you."

Tom led us right up to and into the big entrance chamber of Skeleton Cave. Several men were there, including Mr. Jensen who was arguing with Uncle Mark. "What kind of a marshal are you? My two boys are lost in that cave and it is your job to find them."

"I can only push the search party so far," Uncle Mark

said patiently. "We haven't had a wink of sleep in two days. Just give us a few hours to get some rest and then we'll continue the search."

Tom walked up to Uncle Mark. He tapped his finger on his forehead. "My great brain has figured out a way to save Frank and Allan and Lady," he said.

Mr. Jensen pushed Tom to one side. "Get that boy out of here," he ordered Uncle Mark. "This is no time for kids and their kid games."

"Don't you dare shove that boy again," Uncle Mark said. Then he looked at Tom. "If you have any idea how to rescue the Jensen boys, please tell me."

"First we have to go to the Jensen place," Tom said. "Then we have to stop at the meat market."

"Of all the infernal nonsense," Mr. Jensen said. "Marshal, get this boy out of here and get on with the search."

"Look Mr. Jensen," Uncle Mark said sharply, "I'm grabbing at straws and so should you by this time." Then he took off his holster and revolver and handed them to Don Huddle, the blacksmith. "I'm making you a deputy marshal, Don," he said. "Stand guard and don't let anybody go into that cave, and that goes for Mr. Jensen too." Then he looked down at my brother. "Let's go, Tom."

"J.D. and Brownie have to come too," Tom said.

I was thrilled and grateful to be included. Tom led the way to the Jensen home and around to Lady's doghouse in the backyard.

"Lady is in heat," Tom said. "I want Brownie to get inside her doghouse and smell that Lady is in heat."

Brownie began to whimper as he entered the doghouse and smelled around in it.

Then Tom led the way to the Deseret Meat Market.

58

"We want a big piece of beef liver," he told Mr. Thompson, the butcher.

Uncle Mark tried to pay for the meat. Mr. Thompson refused to take any money when told the liver was going to be used to try and rescue the Jensen brothers.

"It doesn't make sense," Mr. Thompson said, "but take it with my blessing."

When we returned to the entrance chamber of the cave, Mr. Jensen was sitting on a rock, crying. Tom sat down on the ground. He rubbed the piece of liver on the soles of his shoes and then handed the meat to Uncle Mark.

"Brownie has the scent of Lady being in heat," he told Uncle Mark. "He will find Lady for us in the cave, and Frank and Allan will be with her. We will stop every once in a while and rub the liver on the soles of our shoes. This will give Brownie a scent to lead us back out of the cave."

Uncle Mark grinned as he sat down and rubbed liver on the soles of his shoes. "The next time I need a Sherlock Holmes," he said, "I'll know where to go."

Papa came into the cave as Uncle Mark was lighting a lantern. He looked at Tom and then at Uncle Mark. "What is going on here?" he asked.

"Tom has figured out a way to find the Jensen boys if they are alive," Uncle Mark answered.

"You don't think for a minute I'm going to let my son go into that cave without a search party, do you?" Papa demanded.

"We are depending on Lady being in heat to give Brownie the scent that will enable him to lead us to her," Uncle Mark explained. "If I take a search party along, it will distract the dog. And I've got to take Tom with me so Brownie will have somebody he knows and trusts along."

"Don't worry, Papa," Tom said confidently. "We'll be back in two shakes of a lamb's tail with Frank and Allan and Lady."

"If anything happens to you, son," Papa said—and I knew how concerned he must be when he called Tom son—"I'll never forgive myself."

"Nothing is going to happen to me," Tom said. "Can we go now please?"

"Are you afraid?" Papa asked.

"Heck, no," Tom said as if becoming impatient with Papa.

Papa looked at Uncle Mark. "I know you wouldn't do this if you didn't think it safe," he said.

"I can't deny there is some risk," Uncle Mark said, "but we've got to think of those boys in there."

Papa knelt in the dirt and embraced Tom. "Good luck, son," he said and his voice was husky.

I wasn't the least bit scared. Maybe it was my confidence in my brother's great brain. Maybe it was my confidence in my dog. I felt no fear at all as I watched Uncle Mark enter the passageway to the cave. In one hand he held a rope leash which he had attached to Brownie and in the other he carried a lighted lantern. Tom followed carrying the piece of liver wrapped in the brown paper they had gotten from the meat market.

They had been gone about fifteen minutes when Mrs. Jensen and Mamma came into the entrance chamber of the cave. Mrs. Jensen walked over to where her husband was still sitting on a rock.

"What were the marshal and Tena's two boys doing around Lady's doghouse?" she asked.

Mr. Jensen looked up at his wife. "The marshal thinks

the Fitzgerald boy's dog might find Lady from her scent in the cave," he said. "There is still hope, my dear."

Mamma just stood there staring at Papa but saying nothing.

"I had to let the boy try it," Papa finally said. "Mark said it was the only way."

Mamma still said nothing as she walked over and put her hand in Papa's.

Just then Sweyn came running into the cave's chamber. He looked at Papa and Mamma and then sat down on the chamber floor beside me.

"What's going on?" he whispered.

I told him.

Sweyn shook his head when I finished. "Old T.D. sure has courage," he said. "I wouldn't venture into that cave for anything."

"I would have gone with them if Uncle Mark had asked me," I said.

"Like fun you would," Sweyn said loudly. "They say there are monsters and big snakes in the cave."

"That will be enough of that," Papa said sternly as Mamma made the sign of the cross.

Don Huddle, who was standing guard over the entrance chamber of the cave, let Mrs. Olsen and Mrs. Winters enter. They were Mrs. Jensen's next-door neighbors. They were carrying a big wicker basket between them. They set the basket down in the middle of the chamber and removed a tablecloth from it. The basket was filled with sandwiches, glasses, and two big jugs of milk.

I knew the way Papa and Mamma were feeling at that moment they would have rather had a cup of coffee than anything. But Mrs. Olsen and Mrs. Winters were Mormons and the Mormons never drank coffee because it was against their religion, just as they never drank tea or any kind of alcoholic beverages or ever smoked any kind of tobacco. All the grown-ups in the chamber except Mr. and Mrs. Jensen accepted a sandwich and a glass of milk from the two ladies. Then Mrs. Winters finally coaxed them into having a sandwich and a glass of milk.

All the adults had been served and it was now time for Sweyn and me to dive into the basket and gorge ourselves on ham and roast chicken and roast beef sandwiches and then top it off with a glass of milk.

After we had eaten our fill, time began moving so slowly that it seemed as if the whole world had come to a halt. I asked Papa the time so many times that he threatened to send me home if I asked him again. But after three hours had passed, Papa himself began looking at his watch every few minutes. He became so nervous that Mamma got suspicious.

"Is there anything you haven't told me?" she asked.

"Mark did say there was some risk," Papa admitted.

I thought at first Mamma would start crying, but she didn't. She put her hand in Papa's and stood straight and brave.

Another hour passed very slowly. Mrs. Jensen began crying as her husband held her in his arms, trying to comfort her. Mamma stood staring at the entrance to the passageway. Papa paced nervously back and forth.

Then Don Huddle left his guard post at the entrance to the cave and walked over to Papa. "We will give them another hour, Fitz," he said, "and if they don't come back by then, we'll send a search party in for them."

Sweyn shook his head as he whispered to me, "Maybe old T.D. is a goner."

I thought I heard a dog bark. Then I was sure of it. I jumped to my feet.

"That's Brownie!" I shouted.

We all ran to the entrance to the passageway. I could now hear both Brownie and Lady barking. Then I saw a flicker of light down the passageway.

Sweyn slapped me on the shoulder. "Old T.D. and his great brain did it!" he shouted.

"T.D. my eye," I said, feeling left out of the glory. "What good would his great brain have been without my dog?"

Mrs. Jensen clasped her hands in prayer. "Please, God," she prayed, "let my sons be with them."

Then we heard Uncle Mark shout, "All safe and sound! I'm going to release the dogs now. They are tearing my arm off."

Brownie and Lady came running into the chamber a moment later. Brownie ran over to me. I knelt and put my arms around him as he licked my face and barked happily. Then he broke away from me. He barked at Lady. They ran out of the cave together. The sight of the two dogs coming out of the cave brought a cheer from the waiting crowd outside.

Inside the chamber everything was just about as mushy as it could get as Uncle Mark, Tom, Frank, and Allan came out of the passageway. Nobody waited for Uncle Mark to untie the rope around their waists. Frank and Allan kept blinking their eyes as their mother and father hugged and kissed them. I guess the light hurt their eyes after being in darkness so long. Papa and Mamma were fussing over Tom as if he'd just returned from a long sea voyage. Sweyn was running around patting everybody on the back as if he were

64

responsible for the rescue. Uncle Mark and Don Huddle were slapping each other on the shoulders and laughing loudly. The rest of the people in the chamber were hugging each other, shaking hands; pounding each other on the back, and carrying on like you never saw. My dog had made the rescue possible, and nobody was paying any attention to me.

Tom no sooner got the rope off his waist than Mr. Jensen picked him up and put my brother on his shoulder. He carried Tom out of the chamber with the rest of us following. The crowd outside began to applaud and cheer as they saw Mr. Jensen and Tom and Frank and Allan. Several men got so excited they began shooting their revolvers in the air. Mr. Jensen held up one hand for silence. The crowd became quiet immediately.

"My sons owe their lives to this brave boy on my shoulder!" Mr. Jensen shouted.

The crowd went wild then, whistling, shouting, applauding as if Tom were some kind of a king.

Then Uncle Mark held up his hands for silence. "The Jensen boys are exhausted and very hungry," he shouted. "I could use some rest myself. Please make way for us and let us go home."

The crowd made a pathway as Mr. Jensen put Tom down. They kept cheering and reaching out to pat my brother on the shoulder as we walked down Cedar Ridge with Mamma and Papa. They even followed us home and stood in the street in front of our house.

I followed Papa, Mamma, Sweyn, and Tom into our parlor. Tom walked to the big bay window and looked out at the crowd in the street.

"I guess I'll have to speak to them," he said.

Papa winked at Mamma. "I think that would be a good idea, T.D.," he said.

I started to follow Tom out to the front porch to share in the bows because it was my dog.

"Let him go alone, J.D.," Papa said. "This is his day."

Far be it from me to be jealous, but this was getting to be sickening. Everybody was hailing my brother as a hero when my dog was the real hero. My dog couldn't take any bows, but as his owner I could have taken a few for him.

The crowd gave a mighty cheer as Tom appeared on the front porch. My brother held up his hands for silence. The crowd obeyed him.

"When I learned that Uncle Mark and the search party were about ready to give up the search as hopeless," he said, with about as much modesty as a plucked chicken hanging in the window of the Deseret Meat Market, "I knew the only way to save Frank and Allan and Lady was to put my great brain to work. I would have done it sooner but I wanted to give the grown-ups every chance. When they failed, I knew it was up to me to save the day. And now, folks, please go home. I've got to rest up my great brain so it will be ready the next time something happens which you grown-ups can't solve."

I expected the crowd of grown men and women to throw rotten eggs at Tom after the way he had insulted them. Instead they cheered and applauded.

Papa looked at Mamma and smiled. "What a modest son we have," he said.

"You can't deny," Mamma said, "that his great brain did make fools out of Mark and the rest of the men in this town."

"What about my dog?" I asked, feeling completely left out.

66

Papa and Mamma had no ears for me as their conquering hero came back into the parlor. They fussed over him right up until it was time for us boys to go to bed that night. I only had a little brain but it only took a little brain to figure it all out. If I hadn't been playing with Brownie and making my dog bark when Tom was up in his loft, The Great Brain might never have got the idea of using my dog for the rescue.

One other thing bothered me. I asked Tom about it as we were getting undressed for bed that night.

"What did you mean when you said it would cost you a fortune if Frank and Allan and Lady were not found alive?" I asked.

Tom held his undershirt half over his head and peered out of it like a photographer taking a picture.

"It's a business deal I made with them," he answered.

"What kind of a deal?" I asked because I was curious.

Tom whipped off his undershirt. "That is none of your business," he said.

The only business deal I knew about with Frank and Allan was that I would get the pick of the litter from Brownie and Lady's pups. I couldn't help feeling before I fell asleep that somehow and in some way I was going to end up with the short end of the deal. And, oh, how I wished I had a great brain like my brother's so I could figure it out.

CHAPTER FOUR

Abie Glassman Finds a Home

ABIE GLASSMAN AND HIS peddler's wagon arrived in Adenville just a few days after The Great Brain
had saved the day. Abie traveled all over southwestern Utah
with his peddler's wagon, selling merchandise to ranchers,
farmers, and people living in small towns. Everybody, including children, called him Abie, because he was that type of a
man—friendly, kind, and gentle.

The wagon was painted white and had signs on both
sides of it reading THE TRAVELING EMPORIUM. It was con-
structed so it could be opened to display merchandise on
both sides. The tailgate let down, forming steps leading into
the wagon. The aisle down the center of the wagon had

shelves on both sides containing merchandise. Everything from hairpins to coyote traps was on display.

Tom and I were sitting on our back porch, polishing Mamma's silverware for Sunday's dinner on the Saturday morning Abie arrived in town. We had a bucket of ashes Aunt Bertha had taken from the kitchen range that morning before building a fire in it, a pan of water, and a pile of clean rags. We dipped the rags into the water and then into the bucket of ashes and used this to polish all the stains off the silverware. It was a boring job but one Tom and I had to do every Saturday morning so the silverware would be all clean and sparkling for our Sunday dinner.

Howard Kay came running into our backyard and up onto our back porch. "Abie and his peddler's wagon are here!" he shouted. "He's coming down Main Street right now."

Tom got up and ran to the kitchen door. "Mamma," he shouted, "can we let the silverware go until we've seen Abie and his peddler's wagon?"

"All right, boys, but don't stay too long," Mamma said.

We ran around to Main Street with Howard. Abie and his wagon were just passing in front of our house. There were a couple of dozen kids following it. We joined them and

followed the wagon to a vacant lot owned by Calvin Whitlock, the banker, who always let Abie use it when in town.
By the time we had arrived at the vacant lot there were
about fifty kids with us. We waited patiently while Abie un-
hitched his team and staked them out in the lot.

Abie was a small man with a gray beard and moustache.
He wore a Jewish skull cap and his gray hair protruded from
beneath it.

"I think we are ready now, boys," he said as he let down
the tailgate of the wagon. "Get in line and don't push,
please."

Every year since I could remember, Abie had let us
kids see the inside of the wagon first. This was only half of
the treat when Abie came to town. He always stationed himself outside the wagon with a glass jar filled with jaw-
breaker candy, the kind that lasts a long time. As we came out
of the wagon each kid was given a jaw-breaker.

Tom and I saw the inside of the wagon and received
our jaw-breaker and then returned to our job of polishing
silverware on our back porch. Sweyn was lucky. Mamma said
he was too old to have to polish silverware anymore.

When Papa came home that evening, he told Mamma
he'd invited Abie for Sunday dinner. A Sunday dinner in our
house without guests was unusual. Mamma always prepared
for guests because half the time Papa forgot to tell her that
he had invited people for Sunday dinner. One Sunday Papa
had forgotten to tell Mamma that he'd invited Chief Tav-
Whad-Im and the chief's two sons and their squaws for Sunday dinner. The Indian was the chief of the Pa-Roos-Its band
of the Paiute tribe that lived on the Indian reservation near
Adenville. The chief's name translated into English meant
Chief Rising Sun, and you would have thought the way the

70

chief and his sons and their squaws ate that Sunday that none of them ever expected to see the sun rise again. It was a good thing Mamma had prepared for guests that day.

Sunday morning we all went to the Community Church. There were only two churches in Adenville, the Mormon Tabernacle and the Community Church. All the Catholics and Protestants in town went to the Community Church. Once in a while a Catholic missionary priest came to Adenville to baptize Catholic babies, marry Catholics, and hold Confessions and Mass in the Community Church. And once a year the Reverend Ingle came to town and held a revival meeting in a big tent on the campground, lasting one week. All the Protestants in town went to the revival meeting.

When we returned from church, Tom, Sweyn, and I quickly changed into our old clothes. Then we waited on the back porch until Papa had changed clothes and come out wearing his overalls. This was the day of the week when we made ice cream, and everybody helped.

We followed Papa down to our icehouse which was located next to our barn. Papa had our icehouse filled every winter with big cakes of ice two feet wide and four feet long, which were brought from a lake in the mountains. The ice was covered with two feet of sawdust so it wouldn't melt during the summer. Papa took a scoop shovel from a nail on the wall in the icehouse and shoveled away the sawdust down to the ice. Then he used a crowbar to pry one of the big cakes of ice loose. Sweyn was ready with the two-man ice saw and helped Papa cut off a cake of ice for our icebox and a cake of ice to use to make ice cream. Tom and I used the ice tongs to drag the cakes of ice outside while Papa and Sweyn covered up the ice in the icehouse again with sawdust. Papa carried one cake of ice with ice tongs and Tom and Sweyn the other

71

cake, to our backyard. We washed the sawdust off of both cakes of ice with our garden hose. Papa carried one cake into the kitchen and put it in the icebox. Tom and Sweyn put the other cake into a wooden tube and began chopping it up with ice picks.

Mamma had the ingredients for making chocolate ice cream poured into the freezer bucket by this time. Sweyn carried the freezer from the kitchen to the back porch. He and Tom packed the freezer with ice and salt. I folded two gunnysacks and placed them on top of the freezer. It was my job to sit on the freezer and hold it steady while Tom and Sweyn took turns turning the handle which made the freezer bucket go around and around in the ice. When the handle got a little hard to turn, Tom called Mamma and told her he thought the ice cream was done. Nobody knew better than Mamma that the ice cream wasn't hard enough, but she never let on. Sweyn uncovered the top of the freezer bucket and wiped the lid off with a towel. Mamma dipped a spoon into the ice cream and tasted it.

"It isn't done, boys," she said.

"Looks done to me," Tom said.

There was nothing Mamma could do but let Tom and then Sweyn and me taste a spoonful of the ice cream.

"You are right, Mamma," Tom said. "It isn't done."

Sweyn put the lid back on the freezer bucket and repacked the top with ice and salt. I took up my position. We all knew Mamma wouldn't stand for any more nonsense. My brothers kept turning the handle until they knew the ice cream was frozen just right.

"It is ready for sure now, Mamma," Tom sang out.

Mamma came out to the porch carrying a big bread pan and three spoons. Sweyn uncovered the freezer bucket. Just

72

as Mamma started to remove the dasher from the bucket, Tom began to whistle.

"What are you whistling about?" Sweyn asked.

"Just thinking about cleaning off the dasher makes me so happy I feel like whistling," Tom answered.

This was one time, I thought to myself, that Seth Smith and Pete Hanson were going to be left out. Every Sunday since school let out both of them had shown up just as Mamma was about to take the dasher out.

"Hello, boys"—Mamma's voice dashed my hopes—"you are just in time."

I turned around. Standing on the porch steps were Seth and Pete with their mouths watering.

Mamma pulled the dasher from the bucket, scraping some ice cream off the blades but still leaving a generous amount. She put the dasher in the bread pan. We had to wait until she went into the kitchen to get spoons for Seth and Pete.

"All right, boys," Mamma said as we crowded around the porch table with the bread pan and dasher in the center of it. "One for the money, two for the show, three to get ready, and away you go!"

Tom with his great brain knew the parts of the dasher to scrape to get the biggest spoonfuls of ice cream. But I managed to give a fair account of myself until the dasher was clean. Then we tipped the bread pan to scoop up the ice cream that had fallen or melted off the dasher.

I got suspicious as I watched Tom walk arm in arm down our porch steps with Seth and Pete as Sweyn repacked the top of the freezer with ice and salt. It just wasn't like my brother to be so bighearted about sharing the dasher with his two friends every Sunday. I followed them until they went

74

around the corner of our woodshed and stopped. I craned my neck and listened.

"Here's my penny," I heard Pete say.

"And mine," Seth said.

"What about next Sunday?" Tom asked.

"What kind you going to have?" Pete asked.

"Pineapple," Tom said. "And you both know Mamma makes the best pineapple ice cream in town."

"We'll be here," Pete said. "Same time. Same signal."

"Right," Tom said. "When you hear me whistling, come to the back porch."

I wanted to run around the corner of the woodshed and denounce my brother for being a crook. I restrained myself until Seth and Pete had left.

"I heard everything," I said to Tom as he came around the corner of the woodshed. "I'm going to tell Mamma. And, boy, when I tell Sweyn, will he give it to you."

"J.D.," Tom said, putting his arm around my shoulder, "I'm not going to try to influence you one way or another. But if you tell Mamma, she is going to insist I give Seth and Pete back the pennies I've collected so far. And knowing Mamma, she will also insist I invite Seth and Pete every Sunday, because their folks are too poor to have ice cream except on special occasions. And Seth is more your friend than he is mine because he is nearer your age. Am I right?"

"I guess that is what Mamma would do all right," I admitted. "But you swindled Sweyn and me."

"How?" Tom asked.

"We would both get more ice cream off the dasher without Pete and Seth digging in," I answered.

"No, you wouldn't," Tom said. "Did you notice I always whistle before and not after Mamma takes the dasher from

75

the freezer bucket? That is so she will see Pete and Seth. You don't think Mamma would leave that much ice cream on the dasher just for you and me and Sweyn, do you?"

"I guess not," I said. "So I won't tell Mamma but I am going to tell Sweyn.

"Go ahead," Tom said. "You will just be cutting off your nose to spite your face. He will want to make as much money on the deal as I do. That means we'll have to take on two more customers. You know the freezer holds just enough ice cream for Sunday dinner, especially when we have guests. Mamma can't leave any more ice cream on the dasher than she does now. It will simply mean less ice cream off the dasher for you every Sunday."

Tom dropped his hand from my shoulder. He looked steadily into my eyes. "As I said, J.D., I'm not going to try to influence you one way or another. I'm going to leave the decision strictly up to you."

I watched him as he walked toward the back porch, leaving me alone to make the decision. He hadn't tried to bribe me or blackmail me. With his great brain I knew he could have influenced me, but he didn't even try. He had treated me as an equal and left the decision strictly up to me. Acting strictly on my own, I decided not to tell Mamma or Sweyn.

After Sunday dinner that day Tom, Sweyn, and I followed Papa and Abie Glassman into the parlor. We listened fascinated as Abie told Papa all the places he'd been during the past year and the things he'd seen and heard. Papa made notes of items he thought would be of interest to the subscribers of the *Adenville Weekly Advocate*. Abie appeared to me not to be his usual cheerful self. Papa also must have noticed it.

"You look worried, Abie," Papa said. "Do you need any money?"

Papa didn't have any money because Mamma said he didn't know beans about trying to save a dollar. But Papa knew he could send Abie to see Calvin Whitlock.

Abie stared at the Oriental rug on the floor. "It isn't money that worries me," he said. "It is just that I am getting too old to travel around with my wagon."

"Then why do it?" Papa asked.

Abie shrugged his thin shoulders. "What else can I do?"

Papa thought for a moment and then snapped his fingers. "Open a variety store right here in Adenville," he said.

Abie's eyes brightened for a second and then became sad. "I'm afraid it wouldn't pay," he said. "The Mormons naturally buy everything they can at the Z.C.M.I. store and there aren't enough non-Mormons in Adenville to support a variety store. Besides, it would take every cent I have to open a store and if it failed . . ." He did not finish the sentence.

"Nonsense," Papa said. "You are thinking back to the time of Brigham Young when the Mormon leader tried to drive all non-Mormon business out of Utah with his Z.C.M.I. stores. Things have changed, Abie. I am not a Mormon but ninety-five per cent of the subscribers to my newspaper are Mormons and I get all their printing business. Don Huddle, the blacksmith, is not a Mormon. Fred Tanner, who owns the livery stable, is not a Mormon."

Papa was a good talker when it came to settling somebody else's future. I knew Abie didn't have a chance when Papa went to work on him.

"Calvin Whitlock has a vacant frame building on Main Street," Papa said. "He can have a carpenter build some

77

counters and shelves in it and partition off the rear for living quarters."

"But—" Abie started to protest.

"No buts about it," Papa interrupted him. "Let's go see Calvin right now."

When Papa returned home, he told Mamma everything was settled. Abie would open his variety store.

"Just think, Tena," Papa said to Mamma, "after years and years of living and traveling around in that peddler's wagon, at last Abie Glassman has found a home."

CHAPTER FIVE

Greek Immigrant

IT WAS RIGHT AFTER Abie Glassman opened his Adenville Variety Store that Vassillios Kokovinis arrived in town with his mother. He was the first genuine immigrant boy that we had ever seen. His father, George Kokovinis, had come to this country five years before, leaving Mrs. Kokovinis and Vassillios behind in Greece. During those five years Mr. Kokovinis had worked in the coal mines at Castle Rock and saved his money. Then he had come to Adenville and opened the Palace Cafe and sent for his wife and son. He had learned how to speak pretty good English during this time, but his wife and son couldn't speak one word of English when they arrived in Adenville.

I first saw the Greek boy when we were playing Jackass

Leapfrog on the Smiths' vacant lot. He was peering through the fence watching us with big dark eyes. He had an olive complexion and black curly hair. He was wearing a funny hat with a feather in it. He had on green britches with green suspenders and a shirt with a lace collar on it. Nobody but a genuine immigrant boy would have dared to wear an outfit like that in Adenville. He reminded me of a valentine.

We all stopped playing and stared at the Greek boy.

"That's the Greek kid," Sammy Leeds said. "Let's have some fun with him." It was like Sammy to say that because he was a sort of a bully with kids younger and smaller than him.

Howard Kay, Jimmie Peterson, Danny Forester, Andy Anderson, and I followed Sammy over to the fence.

"Come and play, kid," Sammy said, lifting up the fence.

The Greek boy correctly interpreted the invitation and crawled under the fence.

"We are playing Jackass Leapfrog," Sammy said as he led the immigrant boy to the center of the lot. He pushed the Greek boy's head down in position to play leapfrog. "You are the jackass," Sammy said as if the new kid understood English. "Now stay that way."

The rest of us kids lined up with Sammy in the lead.

"Whack the jackass on the rump!" Sammy shouted as he ran and leapfrogged over Vassillios with one hand while he whacked the Greek boy on the rump with his other hand.

The rest of us followed, whacking the jackass on the rump.

"Give the jackass the spurs!" Sammy shouted as he ran and leapfrogged over Vassillios, doubling up his fists and twisting his knuckles in the Greek boy's back.

80

I took my turn but didn't twist my knuckles because I knew the Greek boy wasn't used to the game.

"Chop off the jackass's head!" Sammy shouted as he ran and leapfrogged over Vassillios with one hand and brought the butt of his other hand down on the Greek boy's neck.

The rest of us took our turns.

"Kick the jackass!" Sammy shouted as he leapfrogged over Vassillios and kicked the Greek boy on the rump with the heel of his shoe.

That should have ended the Greek boy's turn at being the jackass. Sammy was in the lead which meant it was his turn now to be the jackass.

"Why should I be the jackass?" Sammy asked with a grin. "This Greek kid don't know from nothing. We'll make him the jackass all the time. Get in line."

I didn't get in line because I didn't think it was fair to make the Greek boy the jackass all the time. I sat down by the fence and watched as Sammy made Vassillios the jackass four straight times. I was glad when I saw Tom and Sweyn coming into the lot. I ran to meet them.

"Sammy isn't playing fair," I told them. "He made the new Greek kid the jackass four times in a row."

Tom walked over and grabbed Sammy by the arm. "If you are going to play Jackass Leapfrog with this new kid, you are going to play fair," he said.

Sammy jerked his arm away. "Why should us American kids get whacked and kicked when we got a Greek kid we can make the jackass all the time?" he asked belligerently.

"It is your turn to be the jackass and you be it," Tom ordered him.

Sammy folded his arms on his chest. "And if I say No?"

81

Tom bent over and picked up a piece of wood which he placed on his shoulder. "You are going to have to fight me," he said, daring Sammy to knock the chip of wood off and start a fight.

Sammy knew Tom could whip him although Sammy was a year older than my brother and bigger. He didn't argue. He walked over and pushed the Greek boy to one side and bent over to be the jackass. Howard Kay and the other kids continued to play with Sammy as the jackass.

I walked with Sweyn and Tom over to where the Greek boy was standing.

Tom pointed at himself. "Me Tom," he said.

The Greek boy pointed at my brother. "Me Tom," he said.

Tom shook his head. "Just Tom," he said.

Again the Greek boy pointed at my brother. "Just Tom," he said. Then he pointed at himself. "Vassillios," he said.

"That is a funny name," Tom said.

"Not half as funny as Just Tom," Sweyn said, laughing.

Tom pointed at me. "That's John," he said. Then he pointed at Sweyn. "Him Sweyn."

Vassillios nodded at if he understood. He pointed at Tom. "Just Tom," he said. Then he pointed at me. "That's John," he said. Then he pointed at Sweyn. "Him Sweyn," he said.

"He thinks those are our names," Sweyn said as he chuckled. Then he slapped Tom on the back. "How are you, Just Tom?"

Tom didn't laugh. "This kid is going to need a lot of help," he said. "He doesn't understand one word of English."

We played Jackass Leapfrog until everybody had been

the jackass. Then we taught Vassillios how to play Kick the Can until it was lunchtime.

Tom pointed at his mouth and then rubbed a hand over his stomach. "Time to eat," he said to the Greek boy.

Vassillios smiled as he grabbed Tom by the arm and began pulling my brother toward the street. Tom tried to explain it was time for us to go home for lunch, but the Greek boy wouldn't let go.

"You might as well go with him and see what he wants," Sweyn said.

I followed Tom and Vassillios down Main Street and up an alley to the rear entrance of the Palace Cafe. We entered the big kitchen.

Mrs. Kokovinis was peeling potatoes. Mr. Kokovinis, wearing a high white chef's hat, was just putting two big steaks on the grill. Everything in the kitchen smelled good.

Vassillios began to jabber in Greek. I guessed he was telling his parents about playing Jackass Leapfrog because he bent over and whacked himself on the rump. Then he put his hand on Tom's shoulder.

"Just Tom," he said. Then he nodded toward me. "That's John."

Mr. Kokovinis walked over to Tom and held out his hand. "You will be my son's friend?" he asked as if it was important to him.

"Yes, Mr. Kokovinis," Tom said as they shook hands. "But tell him my name is Tom and not Just Tom and my brother's name is John and not That's John."

Mr. Kokovinis spoke in Greek to his son. I heard my name and Tom's name mentioned in English. Then he spoke to Tom.

"In English you say my son's name as Basil."

83

"Basil," said Vassillios, nodding his head.

Then Basil began jabbering in Greek to his father.

Mr. Kokovinis looked at Tom. "My son wants you and your brother to have lunch with him," he said. "How about a bowl of chili and a piece of coconut cream pie?"

My mouth began to water. I had never eaten in a restaurant before.

"All right," Tom said, "but only if you let Basil have lunch at our house sometime."

Mr. Kokovinis appeared surprised. "You invite my son to your house for lunch?"

"Don't you want him to come to my house?" Tom asked as if puzzled.

"Of course," Mr. Kokovinis said. "It will be an honor. You be my son's friend and I'll give you anything you want."

Poor Mr. Kokovinis, I thought to myself, you had better watch out or my brother and his great brain will take your cafe away from you.

"I'll be Basil's friend," Tom promised. "I'll make a hundred per cent American kid out of him."

"You are a good boy," Mr. Kokovinis said, and looked as if he was about to cry.

Then Mrs. Kokovinis began jabbering in Greek and pointing at the stove where the two steaks were burning on the grill. Her husband ran to the stove and turned the two steaks over.

Tom asked permission to use the telephone in the front part of the cafe. He called Mamma and explained to her why we wouldn't be home for lunch.

Then we sat down in a booth with Basil. His father brought us bowls of chili and each of us a whopping big piece of coconut cream pie and a glass of milk. After eating, we went back into the kitchen. We had to wait for about half an hour because Mr. Kokovinis was busy cooking and waiting on customers. Finally he was free for a few minutes. I had been wondering why Tom was sticking around instead of going out to play with Basil.

My brother very solemnly informed Mr. Kokovinis there were certain things Basil would need, like marbles, to be able to play with other kids, and these things would cost money. Tom generously offered to help Basil get these things. I was bug-eyed as I watched Mr. Kokovinis hand Basil a whole silver dollar. I couldn't help thinking he would have saved time by just giving the dollar to Tom.

I wasn't surprised when we left the cafe with Basil and Tom walked right by the Z.C.M.I. store and Abie's variety store. He led the Greek boy straight up to our bedroom. Tom pulled the homemade chest containing his possessions from beneath our bed. Then he got his bank out of the clothes closet. He shook out a dollar's worth of change in nickels and dimes and pennies. Then he sat cross-legged on the floor with Basil sitting opposite him. He pushed the dollar in change across to Basil and held out his hand. Basil understood. He gave Tom the silver dollar.

Then began the greatest swindle in pantomime in Adenville's history. Tom took twenty of his agate marbles and one flint taw and put them in an empty tobacco sack. He handed the sack to Basil and helped himself to fifteen cents of Basil's money. Then he took out his homemade slingshot from his chest and handed it to Basil and helped himself to another ten cents. The one-sided trading continued until Tom had gotten rid of all his old junk and had all but ten cents of the dollar Mr. Kokovinis had given Basil.

I guess my brother's conscience must have been hurting

him, because when we left our house, he took Basil and me to the Z.C.M.I. store and blew us each to a penny stick of licorice. I was positive that Mr. Kokovinis would denounce my brother as a cheat and a swindler when he found out what Tom had done as we trooped into the kitchen of the cafe. I couldn't believe my eyes as Basil showed his father all the junk Tom had unloaded on him, and Mr. Kokovinis just stood there looking as if my brother was Basil's guardian angel.

Then we went into the alley. Tom drew a ring in the dirt and began teaching Basil how to play marbles.

"You aren't going to play him for keeps are you?" I asked, wondering if Mr. Kokovinis would be so pleased when he discovered that all the marbles my brother had sold his son had been won back by Tom.

"Of course not," Tom said as if I'd hurt his feelings. "I only play for keeps with kids who can shoot as good as I do."

Mr. Kokovinis kept coming to the kitchen door every few minutes to watch with a big smile on his face. The smile became even wider when we stopped playing marbles and Tom began teaching Basil how to speak English. They sat on the steps leading to the kitchen.

Tom pointed at his nose. "Nose," he said.

Basil pointed at his nose. "Nose," he said.

By the time Tom and I had to leave to go home and do our chores before super, Basil had learned the English names for most of the parts of his body.

As I walked home with Tom I couldn't help putting into words what I'd been thinking all afternoon.

"Don't you feel any shame at all?" I asked.

"Shame for what?" Tom asked and looked surprised.

86

"For unloading all your old junk on Basil and swindling him out of ninety cents," I said.

"It wasn't junk," Tom said, and there was anger in his voice. "It was all stuff American kids have. Take my old slingshot which I sold to Basil. Can his father make him one? No. Can Basil make one? No."

"But they could have bought a store slingshot for a dime," I said.

"How many kids in this town own a store-bought slingshot?" Tom asked. "If Basil bought one, it would make the other kids jealous of him."

It was true but I wasn't through. "How about the secondhand marbles you sold him? You charged him as much as he would have had to pay for new ones at the store."

"I guess your little brain is too little to understand," Tom said as if I'd stabbed him in the back. "I've taken on a task no other kid in town would touch—teaching Basil English and how to be a good American kid. You saw how happy I made Basil. You saw how happy I made his father and mother. Would you rather I abandon Basil and let the other kids in town make a fool out of him the way they did playing Jackass Leapfrog? I think you owe me an apology, J.D."

I was now the one who felt ashamed. Here my brother was doing a wonderful, kind, and generous thing and I hadn't realized it.

"I'm sorry, T.D.," I said.

Becoming an American kid was not an easy thing for Basil or for my brother Tom. The other kids made Basil the butt of jokes and the goat in any game they played when Tom wasn't around. One day I found that Sammy Leeds and a bunch of kids had formed a circle around Basil on Smiths' vacant lot and were shouting at him: "Greasy Greek from Greece!" When Tom found out that Sammy Leeds had started it, he gave Sammy a bloody nose and a black eye in a fight.

That night after supper as Tom sat on the floor in the parlor, he looked up at Papa. "Why does Sammy Leeds hate Basil so much?" he asked. "Basil never did anything to him."

Papa laid aside a book he was reading. "He gets it from his father," Papa said. "His father is always complaining about immigrants coming to this country and taking jobs away from Americans."

"But Sammy's grandfather was an immigrant," Tom said.

"When you come right down to it," Papa said, "we are all immigrants except the Indians. What men like Mr. Leeds fail to understand is that it is the mingling of the different cultures, talents, and know-how of the different nationalities which will one day make this the greatest nation on earth. All intolerant persons must have somebody or something to hate. Mr. Leeds is an intolerant person who hates immigrants."

"I'm sure if it wasn't for Sammy the other kids would leave Basil alone," Tom said. "Basil has got to learn how to fight so he can whip Sammy."

"But Sammy is older and bigger than Basil," Papa said.

"Sammy is older and bigger than me, but I can whip him," Tom said.

Papa just smiled as he picked up his book and resumed his reading.

Tom and I were weeding the vegetable garden a couple of days later when Howard Kay came running into our backyard.

88

"Sammy and his pals have got Basil down by the river and are scaring him to death!" Howard shouted.

"Show me where," Tom said as he jumped to his feet.

We ran all the way to the river where Howard led us along a path through some bushes and into a clearing.

Sammy, Danny Forester, Pete Hanson, and Jimmie Peterson were dressed in their Indian suits and had their faces painted with red crayons. They had Basil tied to a tree in the middle of the clearing. They had piled dead brush around Basil as if they were going to burn him at the stake. They were dancing around the tree, letting out Indian war cries as they waved homemade tomahawks in the air. Basil was screaming and looked as if his eyes would pop right out of his head.

Tom ran across the clearing and grabbed Sammy. He knocked Basil's tormenter down with one punch on the jaw. Sammy's three friends started for Tom. I stepped in front of them.

"You gang up on Tom and I'll get Sweyn to knock your blocks off!" I threatened them.

Howard and I ran to help Basil as the three backed down. We pulled the brush away and untied the Greek boy. Basil was crying hysterically. I couldn't blame him. A Greek boy in a strange country must have thought for sure he was going to be burned at the stake. As soon as we got Basil untied he ran screaming toward town as if a real war party of Indians were chasing him.

Sammy was now on his feet, watching. "Look at the cry baby," he said. "Look at Mamma's boy running crying home to Mamma." Then he looked at Tom. "Are you going to protect that little sissy and do all his fighting for him the rest of your life?" he asked with a sneer on his face.

89

I thought Tom would haul off and knock Sammy down again. Instead he began to nod his head slowly. "You are right, Sammy," he said. "If Basil wants to be an American, he's got to learn to do his own fighting."

Danny Forester stepped up close to Tom. "We weren't going to hurt him," he said. "We were just having a little fun."

"I know it," Tom said, "and you know it. But Basil didn't. But that doesn't excuse him for being such a cry baby."

It was midafternoon before Tom and I finished weeding the vegetable garden. Sweyn had got out of the dirty job because he had to cut the grass. Mamma came out to inspect the garden. She was satisfied and said that we could go play. We went to the rear entrance of the Palace Cafe. We could see Basil's face pressed against a window in the apartment above the cafe where the family lived. Tom marched into the kitchen, with me following him. Mr. Kokovinis was in the kitchen alone.

"Can Basil come out to play?" Tom asked.

Mr. Kokovinis' tall chef's hat wobbled as he shook his head. "That bad boy Sammy Leeds and those other bad boys hurt and scared my son," he said. "Basil don't play with them anymore."

"He can't just stay upstairs with his mother," Tom said. "If he does, what Sammy said is true."

"What did that bad boy say about my son?" Mr. Kokovinis asked.

"He said Basil was a cry baby and a Mamma's boy," Tom said, "and in America there is nothing worse a kid can be."

"My son is no coward," Mr. Kokovinis said. "But he

doesn't understand American ways. He stays home until he does."

"How can you make an American out of him if he stays home?" Tom asked. "He's got to learn how to play the way American kids play. He's got to learn how to take it as well as dish it out. He's got to learn to fight. He's got to fight Sammy and keep on fighting until he can lick him."

"But this Sammy is older and bigger than my son," Mr. Kokovinis protested.

"He is older and bigger than me and I can lick him," Tom said. "I kept on fighting Sammy until I could whip him."

Mr. Kokovinis looked surprised. "You mean you fought this boy when you knew you would lose?" he asked.

"Yes," Tom answered. "I knew the only way to make Sammy stop picking on me was to keep on fighting him until I could lick him. Now we are friends."

"This bully is your friend?" Mr Kokovinis asked.

"Sammy is all right once you get to know him," Tom said. "It isn't his fault that his father hates foreigners."

"I have heard his big-winded father say many untrue things about immigrants," Mr. Kokovinis said. "But I am no foreigner. I am an American citizen and have the papers to prove it. And that makes my wife and son American citizens."

"Just being an American citizen doesn't make a boy a real American, Mr. Kokovinis," Tom said. "Basil has got to prove he deserves to be an American, and the one sure way for him to do it is for him to whip Sammy Leeds."

"His mother will never permit it," Mr. Kokovinis said.

"Then Basil will be a cry baby and Mamma's boy all his life," Tom said. "You can tell Basil for me that I'm through doing his fighting for him. I don't care what Sammy and the other kids do to him from now on."

"Could you come back tomorrow?" Mr. Kokovinis asked.

"Basil knows where I live," Tom said. "If he is afraid to walk from here to my house on account of Sammy Leeds, I don't want him for a friend."

I followed Tom into the alley. I had visions of Mr. Kokovinis coming after us with a big butcher knife, until we reached Main Street.

"Gosh, T.D.," I said, "if Papa knew you talked to a grown-up like that, he would raise Cain. I was expecting Mr. Kokovinis to slap you good and hard for the way you talked to him about his son."

"I had to do it, J.D.," Tom said. "It was the only way to try and save Basil from being a cry baby and a Mamma's boy."

We didn't see Basil for a week. He came into our back-yard as Tom was making me some tin-can stilts.

"What you make, Tom?" he asked.

Tom punched two holes on each side of the cans with a nail and a rock.

"What you make, Tom?" Basil asked again in his broken English.

"We don't talk to cry babies and Mamma's boys," Tom said.

Tom turned the cans over. I stood on top of them. Tom ran a piece of baling wire through the holes near the top of the cans. He made a loop in the wire and measured it to fit my hands. Then he twisted the ends of the wire together.

"Try them, J.D.," he said.

Pulling tight on the wire loops to hold the cans to the soles of my shoes, I began walking around the backyard. The tin-can stilts fit perfectly. All I had to do was wait for it to rain so I could use them.

Basil finally spoke again: "Me no cry baby."

"Then prove it by fighting Sammy," Tom said.

Basil was game. "Me fight Sammy," he said.

I got off the stilts and called Tom to one side. "Sammy will murder him," I whispered.

"I know," Tom said, "but Basil has got to learn to take it. Besides I've got to find out if he knows anything about fighting."

I went to get Sammy. Tom and Basil were waiting in the barn for us when I arrived with Sammy.

"This is to be a fair and square fight," Tom said.

"Before I fight him," Sammy said, "I want to know if you are going to fight me for beating up Basil."

"I'm through fighting for Basil," Tom said.

My brother picked up a chip of wood and placed it on Sammy's shoulder. Basil had seen enough fights to know what to do. He knocked off the chip of wood and got a punch in the nose in return. Then Sammy began clobbering Basil, hitting the Greek boy almost at will.

"Stop it," I pleaded with Tom.

"I've got to see if Basil can take it," Tom said.

Basil's nose was bleeding and one eye starting to swell up as Sammy caught him with a haymaker on the jaw that knocked the Greek boy down. Tom announced the fight was over and Sammy the winner. Sammy left to go brag to his friends about winning the fight. Tom helped Basil to the hydrant in our corral. He held his handkerchief soaked in water on the back of Basil's neck until the Greek boy's nose

94

stopped bleeding. Basil had a lot of courage and could take it all right. He didn't cry, although I knew his nose and eye must be hurting him like the devil.

"You my friend now?" Basil asked.

Tom held out his hand. "Friends," he said.

They shook hands.

"You tell my papa we friends again?" Basil asked.

"Sure," Tom said.

Tom and I didn't know that Basil had sneaked out of the apartment without his mother and father knowing it until we entered the kitchen of the cafe. Mrs. Kokovinis was washing dishes. She took one look at Basil and let out a shriek. She didn't even bother to wipe the soap and water from her hands as she ran to Basil and threw her arms around him.

Tom ignored her. He looked steadily at Mr. Kokovinis. "Basil is no coward or cry baby," he said. "He fought Sammy Leeds. He got whipped because he doesn't know beans about fighting."

I thought Mr. Kokovinis would be angry. Instead he looked pleased. "I knew my son was no coward," he said. "Now this Sammy Leeds, you told me you could beat him. Can you teach my son how to fight so he can beat this boy?"

"I don't know about that, Mr. Kokovinis," Tom said. "It would take a lot of my time because Basil doesn't know how to fight American style."

I thought Mr. Kokovinis was pretty dumb up to this moment, but he proved to me he had sized up my brother.

"You teach my son how to fight American style," he said, "and I will give you one whole dollar the day my son beats Sammy Leeds."

I couldn't help feeling that my brother's great brain had planned it this way when he got Basil to fight Sammy.

95

"As I said," Tom replied, "it will take a lot of my time and should be worth something. It's a deal, Mr. Kokovinis."

At the end of a week of trying to teach Basil how to fight American style, it looked as if Tom would never get that dollar. We were in the barn. Tom was taking off the boxing gloves Papa had given him last Christmas. He was sitting on a bale of hay. He looked mighty dejected.

"I don't know if I can ever make a fighter out of you," he said to Basil. "Why do you keep pushing instead of trying to hit me? You can't hurt me with these boxing gloves on."

"Me try harder next time," Basil promised.

"You don't even know how to stand like a fighter," Tom said with disgust. "You keep acting as if you wanted to wrestle instead of fight."

Tom sat on the floor in the parlor after supper that night, staring into the empty fireplace. I knew he was putting his great brain to work to get that dollar from Mr. Kokovinis. He refused to play dominoes with me and just sat there saying nothing until it was almost our bedtime. Then he got up and walked over to where Papa was reading the mail edition of the *New York World*.

"Why can't Basil learn to use his fists, Papa?" he asked. "I've been trying to teach him how to fight for a week, but all he does is act as if he wanted to wrestle instead of fight."

Papa dropped his newspaper to his lap. "Perhaps it is a natural thing for Basil to want to wrestle," he said. "The Greeks are known as the world's greatest wrestlers. The majority of world champion wrestlers have been Greeks. I imagine that in Greece boys learn wrestling instead of fist-fighting."

"Thanks, Papa," Tom said with a happy look on his face.

The next afternoon Tom spread a horse blanket on the floor of our barn. He told Basil they would wrestle instead of box. I watched bug-eyed as Basil got a headlock on Tom and put my brother down.

I thought Tom's pride would be hurt because he was the champion wrestler for his age in town. Instead he was grinning as he got to his feet.

"Let's try it again," he said.

They sparred for positions, circling each other for a moment. They locked arms. Basil got a wristlock on my brother and before my astonished eyes threw Tom right over his shoulder with a flying mare. He fell on top of Tom and easily pinned my brother's shoulders down.

Tom was laughing as he got up. "Basil can whip Sammy," he said to me.

"Not in a fist fight," I said.

"I'm talking about a rough and tumble fight," Tom said.

Then he put on a pair of boxing gloves. "Now Basil," he said, "I'll fight and you wrestle."

Basil nodded as they squared off. Tom hit Basil a left and a right before they clinched. Then Basil got a headlock on Tom and threw him down. They tried it several times, with Tom getting in a few punches before Basil clinched with him and wrestled him down. Then Tom showed Basil how, in a rough and tumble fight when you get a boy down, you put your knees on his arms to pin him down so you can clobber his face with your fists.

The next morning Tom sent me to get Sammy while he went to get Basil. Sammy was playing One-O-Cat in the Smiths' vacant lot with Danny Forester, Jimmie Peterson, and Pete Hanson. I told Sammy that Basil wanted to fight him again. Sammy did a lot of bragging to his friends on the way to our barn, about how he would clobber Basil again.

Tom and Basil were waiting inside the barn.

"This is going to be a rough and tumble fight," Tom announced. "Anything goes, lumberjack style."

"Suits me," Sammy said, grinning.

Tom put a chip of wood on Sammy's shoulder. Basil knocked it off and got pasted on the jaw in return. They began sparring around.

"Look at him!" Sammy shouted, laughing. "He hasn't even got his fists doubled up."

Sammy led with a left feint to the body and slammed a right cross to Basil's eye. It worked so well that Sammy tried it again and this time threw a right cross to Basil's nose which began to bleed. Then Sammy shot three straight left jabs on Basil's nose making it bleed a lot more. Again Sammy tried a feint to the body and a right cross, but this time Basil clinched with him. Basil got a headlock on Sammy and threw the bigger boy down. Then Basil straddled Sammy as Tom had taught him to do in a rough and tumble fight. Sammy was at Basil's mercy now.

"Paste him!" Tom shouted. "Pay him back for that bloody nose and black eye! Let him have it!"

Basil doubled up his right fist and raised his arm as we all waited breathlessly for him to whale the devil out of Sammy.

"What are you waiting for?" Tom yelled. "This is a rough and tumble fight! Anything goes! Let him have it, Basil!"

But Basil unclenched his fist and got to his feet.

"He just got lucky," Sammy said as he jumped to his feet.

"Have another go at it," Tom said. "I can't declare anybody the winner if you stop now."

The two boys began circling each other. Sammy popped Basil on the nose. The punch made Basil's nose bleed so much the blood was running all over Basil's chin and down on his shirt. Sammy got in three more good punches before Basil could clinch with him. Basil got another headlock on Sammy and threw the bigger boy down. Again Basil straddled Sammy. Again Basil doubled up his right fist.

"Paste him!" Tom shouted. "Let him have it!"

Basil looked at his helpless victim as he slowly unclenched his fist. "Me no mad at you now, Sammy," he said. "Next time you pick on me, I paste you good."

Basil got to his feet. Danny, Jimmie, Pete, and I all crowded around Basil to congratulate him. I guess because Sammy had whipped all three of them several times, it made Basil a sort of hero to them. And I guess Sammy thought it best now to have Basil for a friend instead of an enemy. He got up and held out his hand.

"Friends?" Sammy asked.

"Friends," Basil said as they shook hands.

Sammy must have guessed his defeat was the result of my brother's great brain. "I'll bet you could lick any kid in town in a rough and tumble fight," he said to Basil, but the words were meant for my brother. "I'll bet you could even whip Tom."

"You can't get me to fight him rough and tumble," Tom said, grinning.

"Me only fight to show me no cry baby or Mamma's boy," Basil said, which was quite a mouthful of English for him.

"Three cheers for Basil!" Tom shouted.

99

We all joined in three *hip hip hoorays* for Basil. Then we accompanied him to the hydrant in the corral where Tom stopped the nosebleed with cold packs on Basil's neck. The black eye Sammy had given Basil was almost swollen shut by this time.

I went with Tom and Basil to the Palace Cafe. I was hoping Mrs. Kokovinis wouldn't be in the kitchen, because Basil was a sight. I felt relieved as we entered the kitchen and saw only Mr. Kokovinis. He looked at Basil and shook his head.

"Another one," he said sadly.

"He did it, Mr. Kokovinis!" Tom shouted as he pounded Basil on the back. "Basil whipped Sammy Leeds in a rough and tumble fight and whipped him good!"

Basil was so excited that he began to jabber in Greek as he described the fight to his father. Mr. Kokovinis looked so proud as he listened that I thought he would burst right out of his chef's uniform.

"This is a proud and happy day for the Kokovinis family," Mr. Kokovinis said as Basil finished describing the fight. Then he looked straight at Tom. "And we owe it all to you. Thank you."

Tom's face dropped the distance between a thank you and a dollar. Basil knew my brother well enough by this time to sense what was the matter. He spoke to his father in Greek.

"Of course," Mr. Kokovinis said. "I was so happy I forgot." He put his hand into his pocket and took out a silver dollar which he handed to Tom. "I've been carrying this dollar in my pocket, hoping for the day I could give it to you," he said. "It is very little for the happiness you have brought to me and my son."

"Thank you, Mr. Kokovinis," Tom said as he pocketed the dollar. "And to show you my heart is in the right place,

100

I am going to teach Basil all the English I can before school starts in the fall. And I'm going to be Basil's best friend."

I thought Mr. Kokovinis was going to cry. And if he had known how much it was going to cost him for Tom being Basil's best friend, he probably would have. Now that Tom had made Basil a genuine American kid like the rest of us, it made the Greek boy fair game for my brother's great brain. Right now, I thought to myself, I'll bet Tom is trying to figure out how much to charge Mr. Kokovinis for each new English word he teaches Basil.

CHAPTER SIX

A Wreath for Abie

AUGUST CAME TO ADENVILLE, bringing with it the hottest weather of the year. The heat slowed everybody down. People walked a little slower. Our fathers began crowding us kids at the swimming hole to escape from the heat. Dogs became listless. My dog, Brownie, spent most of his time lying in the shade of a tree or under our back porch. I began to worry about Lady, who was expecting a litter of puppies. Tom had told me that it would take sixty-two days from the day Lady was mated with Brownie before the pups would be born. He assured me that the heat wouldn't stop Lady from having the litter. As always The Great Brain was right. Lady gave birth to a litter of eight beautiful puppies the second

102

week in August. I took Tom's advice and decided to wait until three weeks after the puppies were weaned before taking my pick of the litter.

"They will be bigger then," Tom had told me, "and not dependent on their mother, so I can judge them better."

During the third week in August Abie Glassman fainted in front of the livery stable. He was carried inside by Mr. Tanner and some other men who revived him. Everybody blamed it on the heat.

Abie had earned himself a reputation for being a miser since opening his variety store. It began when he had removed the strong box from his peddler's wagon and placed it in the living quarters of his store. It was a box made from wood with steel bands around it and had a big padlock on it. I guess Abie needed the strongbox when he was traveling around the outlying country and didn't get near a bank only once or twice a year. Everybody who had seen Abie carrying the strongbox into his store had wondered what was in it.

It was just a couple of weeks after Abie opened his store that the rumor got around town the strongbox was filled with gold pieces. A man named Milton Tedford, who worked on the railroad as a brakeman, started the rumor. He had made a purchase in the store and had given Abie a twenty dollar gold piece. He told friends that Abie had gone into the living quarters to make change out of the strongbox. Abie had given Tedford a ten dollar, a five dollar, and a two-and-a-half dollar gold piece in change. As the story was repeated around town people became convinced that the strongbox was filled with gold pieces.

Uncle Mark was worried about the rumor. He told Abie there were always drifters in town who might hear about the strongbox and attempt to rob it. He tried to persuade Abie to put the money in the bank. Abie told Uncle Mark there was nothing to worry about.

Howard Kay was the first one to tell me Abie had a strongbox filled with gold pieces. He had heard his father telling his mother about it. I had run all the way home to tell Tom about it.

Later when I learned Abie had failed to take Uncle Mark's advice and put the money in the bank, I asked Tom why Abie wouldn't.

"What money?" Tom asked as we sat on the back porch steps, waiting until it was lunchtime.

"That strongbox full of gold pieces," I said.

"If anybody tries to rob Abie," Tom said, "he is going to be mighty disappointed."

"How do you know?" I asked.

"I just know, J.D., and that's all," Tom said, and I knew from the way he said it that he wasn't going to tell me any more.

Mamma had tried to buy everything she could from Abie after he'd opened his store. When she sent me to the store on an errand, she always told me to try the variety store first. If Mamma only wanted a small item like a spool of thread, I always went to the variety store. But when she wanted several items, I always went to the Z.C.M.I. store because I knew Mr. Harmon would give me a stick of peppermint candy free. There were never any customers in Abie's store when I did go there. I began to think that Papa had made a big mistake in talking Abie into opening a store in town. And I hoped that people were right and Abie did have a strongbox full of gold pieces, because he sure wasn't doing much business.

104

The second time Abie fainted was just six days after the first time. He fainted in front of the post office. Uncle Mark saw it happen. When he revived Abie, he wanted to take the old man to see Dr. LeRoy.

"A doctor cannot help me," Abie told Uncle Mark.

During supper that evening Papa and Mamma were talking about it.

"I don't understand what Abie meant," Papa said, "unless he meant that he has some kind of incurable disease."

"Dear God I hope not," Mamma said.

The third time Abie fainted was just a few days before school started. It happened right before my eyes. Mamma had sent me to get her a package of needles. I knew Mr. Harmon wouldn't give me any free candy for such a small purchase. I went to the variety store.

"How are your good father and wonderful mother, John?" Abie asked me as he got the package of needles.

"Just fine, thank you," I said.

Abie laid the package of needles on the counter. Then he suddenly pressed his hands to the sides of his head. I became terrified as I watched his eyes roll crazily around and around and saw him fall to the floor. I ran screaming out of the store and didn't stop until I reached the marshal's office. By the time I returned to the store with Uncle Mark some people who had seen me run screaming out of the store had revived Abie. He was sitting in a chair. Again Uncle Mark tried to get Abie to see Dr. LeRoy. Again Abie refused to see the doctor.

I told Mamma about it when I got home.

"Abie must see a doctor," Mamma said when I finished. "Even if he has some incurable disease as you father suspects, at least Dr. LeRoy can give him something for the pain.

I'll get your father to invite Abie for Sunday dinner. That will give your father and me a chance to persuade Abie he must see a doctor."

Papa stopped at the store the next morning to invite Abie for Sunday dinner. There was a CLOSED sign on the door.

"I thought he might be so ill that he closed up the store," Papa told Mamma when he came home for lunch, "so I went around in back and pounded on the rear door. There was no answer. The only explanation I can think of is that Abie went to Salt Lake City to see a specialist or to order some new merchandise for his store."

Mamma sent me to the variety store three days later to get a package of carpet tacks. The CLOSED sign was still on the door. I went to the Z.C.M.I. store to get the tacks. When I told Mamma about it, she got real upset. She telephoned Papa and Uncle Mark to come to our house at once.

I went to tell Tom and Sweyn, who were cleaning the parlor rug. They had it hung on the clothes line and were beating it with broom handles. They were covered with dust, but that didn't stop them from following me into the parlor where Mamma was waiting with Aunt Bertha. Papa and Uncle Mark arrived a moment later.

Nobody sat down as Mamma looked at Uncle Mark. "Did you see Abie leave on the train for Salt Lake?" she asked.

"No," Uncle Mark replied. "I usually meet all trains but that was the day I had to ride out to the Gunderson ranch. Pete Gunderson thought some of his steer had been rustled. We found them after an all-day search in a gully."

"Did anybody see Abie leave?" Mamma asked, and her face was now strained with worry.

"Come to think of it," Papa said, "nobody has mentioned

seeing him leave. And it is strange he didn't tell me so I could put an item about it in the *Advocate*."

"How do we know he did leave?" Mamma asked.

"I see what you are getting at," Uncle Mark said quickly. "There have been quite a few drifters in town lately. One of them might have heard about the strongbox. Putting a CLOSED sign on the door would just be a cover-up to give the robber time for a getaway. Let's go!"

All of us except Aunt Bertha ran all the way to the variety store. Uncle Mark took the butt of his Colt 45 and knocked out a pane of glass in the front door. He reached through the opening and pulled back the barrel bolt lock.

"Locked from the inside," he said with a worried look.

We found Abie lying on his cot in the living quarters of the store. He was holding a Jewish prayer book in his hands, which were clasped on his chest. He was fully dressed, including his Jewish skull cap. His eyes were closed but he was breathing.

"Thank God it wasn't robbery," Papa said. "He is just sick."

"Take him to my house," Mamma said briskly.

"I'm afraid to move him until Dr. LeRoy looks him over," Uncle Mark said. He turned to Sweyn. "Run and get the doctor, Sweyn."

So many people had crowded into the store and living quarters by the time Sweyn returned with Dr. LeRoy that they had to push their way through the crowd. Dr. LeRoy ordered everybody out of the living quarters except Uncle Mark. He pulled the curtains across the doorway to the store so we couldn't see. He and Uncle Mark remained there for what seemed a long time before coming out.

Finally Dr. LeRoy pushed aside the curtains and came

into the store. His eyes were wide and his mouth twisted as if he were in pain.

"Abie is dying of malnutrition," he said in a hoarse whisper.

I grabbed Tom's arm. "What's malnutrition?" I whispered.

"Hunger," Tom answered. "Abie is starving to death."

"Can he be moved?" Mamma asked as tears came into her eyes.

"He must be," Dr. LeRoy said. "He needs immediate care and nursing but I'm afraid . . ." He didn't finish the sentence.

"Bring him home with me," Mamma said.

Uncle Mark wrapped Abie in a blanket and picked the sick man up in his arms. "He's as light as a feather, just skin and bones," Uncle Mark said, his voice choking.

Uncle Mark carried Abie down Main Street to our house, with a crowd of people following. Mamma told him to put Abie in her bedroom. She ordered Aunt Bertha to prepare some broth immediately. Then she sat on the edge of the bed bathing Abie's face with a wet cloth.

When Aunt Bertha brought the hot broth, Mamma tried to spoon feed it to Abie. He spat it out on the bed. Then Dr. LeRoy tried to force the broth down Abie's throat. Abie threw it up.

"I'm afraid we are too late," Dr. LeRoy said sadly.

Mamma cradled Abie's head in her arms. He opened his eyes slowly. A flicker of recognition came into them as he looked at Mamma. His lips moved but no words came. Then he died in Mamma's arms.

Mamma lay his head gently on the pillow. Dr. LeRoy closed Abie's eyelids. Mamma pulled the sheet up over Abie's

head. Then Mamma walked slowly into our parlor which was filled with people. She looked as if she had just lost one of her own loved ones.

"Abie is dead," she said as tears toppled down her cheeks. "Three times he fell carrying his cross, just as Christ did, and we were too blind to see. May God have mercy on us."

Every business in town closed the day we buried Abie. Every man, woman, and child able to walk followed the pine-board coffin to the cemetery. We stood there shamefaced, an entire town, as Reverend Holcomb of the Community Church looked helplessly across the grave at Bishop Aden of the Church of Jesus Christ of Latter-day Saints.

"Read the Christian burial service over him," the Mormon Bishop said as the wind from a threatening cloudburst made his white beard wave back and forth. "I am sure both God and Abie will understand."

We buried Abie with Reverend Holcomb reading the Christian burial service as thunder roared and streaks of lightning stabbed like swords of fire through the sky. The rain broke as the first shovelful of dirt was placed on the pine coffin. Then the cloudburst came, with rain coming down as if dumped from giant buckets in the sky. Not a man, woman, or child left the cemetery until the last shovelful of dirt had been placed on the grave and a big wreath made by all the ladies of the Community and Mormon churches placed upon it. I guess we all stood there praying that the rain would wash away some of the guilt from us.

Uncle Mark and his wife, my Aunt Cathie, accompanied the family and Aunt Bertha back to our house from the cemetery. We removed our wet coats and hats in the side hallway and then all went into the parlor. Everybody sat down as if exhausted except Uncle Mark and us three boys.

110

"If I had only known," Uncle Mark said, "but I had no idea. I thought Abie was doing all right. Calvin Whitlock told me Abie was paying his rent right on the dot. And I heard so much about that strongbox being filled with gold pieces that I believed it until I opened the box and found it empty."

"It wasn't empty," Mamma said. "It contained a man's most priceless possession."

"I don't understand what you mean, Tena," Uncle Mark said as he leaned against the mantlepiece of the fireplace.

"What Tena means," Papa said, "is that the strongbox was a symbol of Abie's pride. To have opened it and let everybody know it was empty would have meant having charity forced upon him. Abie chose to die with Jewish dignity instead of living in the humiliation of charity. It could never have happened if he hadn't been a Jew."

"Nonsense," Uncle Mark said. "There isn't a man or woman in this town who would hold that against a person."

"You don't understand what I meant," Papa said. "We have cowboys who are out of work coming into town all the time. And they are broke. But they know they can live on the free lunches in the saloons and sleep in the livery stable until they find work. And when they do find work and have money, they will come into town and spend money in these saloons and stable their horses at the livery stable. Abie didn't drink. He knew he would never spend any money in a saloon and his pride wouldn't let him go to one to eat a free lunch even when he knew he was starving to death."

"What has that got to do with letting Abie starve to death because he was a Jew?" Uncle Mark demanded. "Abie was my friend and your friend and had all kinds of friends. He

111

knew all he had to do was to ask and we would have given him anything he wanted."

"But he would have had to ask," Papa said.

"I just don't get what you're driving at," Uncle Mark said, shaking his head.

"Let me put it this way," Papa said. "It isn't that we dislike the Jews or mean to be unkind to them. It is just that we don't worry about them the way we worry about other people. I talked to Mr. Thompson at the meat market. He knew Abie had stopped buying meat from him weeks ago, but he didn't worry about it. I talked to Mr. Harmon at the Z.C.M.I. store. He knew Abie had stopped buying groceries from him, but he didn't worry about it. Oh, they had their excuses, saying they had thought Abie had stopped batching and was eating in cafes. But the fact remains we let a man starve to death because nobody worried about a Jew."

"I don't buy that," Uncle Mark said.

"Let us assume," Papa said patiently, "that Dave Teller, who is a bachelor and cooks his own meals, suddenly stopped buying meat from Mr. Thompson. You can bet Mr. Thompson would have made it his business to find out why. And let us assume that Dave Teller suddenly stopped buying groceries from the Z.C.M.I. store. You can bet Mr. Harmon would have worried enough about it to find out why. And let us assume they found out Dave Teller was broke. You can bet they wouldn't have let Dave Teller starve to death. And if Dave Teller had fainted three times, you can bet the people in this town would have insisted on taking Dave to a doctor whether he wanted to go or not. But Abie was a Jew and so nobody worried about him. May God forgive us all."

"I see what you're getting at now," Uncle Mark said. "We are all guilty."

112

Mamma nodded her head as she brushed a tear from her eye with her handkerchief. "God give us strength," she said softly, "to bear our burden of guilt."

Two days after the funeral Mamma sent me to the Z.C.M.I. store to get several items for her. Mr. Harmon, as usual, gave me a stick of peppermint candy. I came out of the store holding the bag of groceries in one hand while I put the stick of candy into my mouth with the other hand. I took a bite of the candy. It burned my mouth and stuck in my throat. I tried to swallow it but couldn't. I spat it out. I threw the candy away and have never been able to eat peppermint candy since.

Tom was sitting on the rail of the corral fence when I got home. I climbed up and sat down beside him. I told him about the peppermint candy.

"It's your guilty conscience, J.D.," he said when I finished. "You helped to kill Abie."

I thought of all the times Mamma had sent me to the store when I should have stopped at the variety store instead of going to the Z.C.M.I. store.

"How was I to know that strongbox wasn't full of gold pieces," I defended myself.

"You are just using that as an excuse like most people in town," Tom said. "Maybe I should have told."

"Told what?" I asked.

"You didn't think my great brain would let me rest until I knew what was in that strongbox, did you?" he asked. "I have known there were no gold pieces in the box for a long time."

"How did you find out?" I asked.

"I went to see Abie and told him I'd overheard two drifters planning to rob him and the strongbox," Tom answered.

113

"You lied," I accused him.

"How else could I find out?" Tom said. "At first Abie just laughed. He stopped laughing when I threatened to call Papa and Uncle Mark so they could make him put the gold in the bank before he got robbed. Then he began to cry."

"To cry?" I asked, bewildered.

"Yes," Tom said. "Then he opened the strongbox and showed me it was empty. He told me it had taken every cent he owned to open the store. Then he made me put my hand on a prayer book and swear I would never tell. He said as long as people thought he had a strongbox full of gold pieces he could remain in Adenville. He said he would have to leave if people found out the strongbox was empty."

"What did he mean?" I asked.

"I thought he meant if people thought he was rich they would respect him more," Tom said. "But I was wrong. It was like Papa said—Abie would rather die than take charity."

"I'd hate to have it on my conscience that I let a man starve to death," I couldn't help saying.

"It wasn't me who let Abie starve to death," Tom said. "I knew there was no gold in the strongbox, but that only meant Abie wasn't a rich man to me. When Mamma sent me to the store, I always went to the variety store first. Many times when Abie didn't have exactly what Mamma wanted, I went all the way back home to ask her if she couldn't use something else Abie had suggested. No, J.D., it wasn't me who let Abie starve to death. It was people like you."

"But you will get all the blame," I said, "when people find out you knew the strongbox was empty all the time."

"The people who didn't buy from Abie and didn't worry about him would love to have somebody to blame for his death," Tom said. "But they are going to have to live with

114

their guilty consciences because I'm never going to tell, and neither are you. Give me your word, J.D., you will never tell."

"Not even Papa and Mamma?" I asked.

"Not even Papa and Mamma," Tom said.

"But you told me," I protested.

"I had to tell somebody, J.D.," Tom said. "I knew I could trust you."

I gave my word and kept it until now.

CHAPTER SEVEN

The New Teacher

SUMMER VACATION CAME to an end. We all went down to the depot to see Sweyn off for Salt Lake City to attend a Catholic academy and boarding school. Mamma was crying. Papa kept clearing his throat. I felt a lump in my throat that wouldn't go up and wouldn't go down. Tom was very quiet. The only one who didn't appear even a little upset was Sweyn.

"Please stop crying, Mamma," he said.

"What if Father O'Malley forgets to meet you at the depot in Salt Lake?" Mamma sobbed.

"You saw the telegram from Father O'Malley saying he would meet me," Sweyn said. "Please stop crying, Mamma. People are staring at us. I'm not a little boy."

Mamma dried her tears with a handkerchief. "You are right, my son," she said. "You are not a little boy. I know I don't have to ask you to promise you will write every week."

The train came. There were kisses, hugs, good-byes, and more tears from Mamma. Sweyn boarded the train. He stood by a window, waving at us as the train pulled out of the station.

I put my arm around Tom's shoulders. "Old S.D. certainly has courage," I said. "He didn't even cry."

"That was an act put on for Mamma and Papa," Tom said. "As soon as the train gets around the bend he will need that extra handkerchief Mamma put in his pocket."

"It is going to be lonesome without S.D. around," I said.

"That is life, J.D.," Tom said. "When I graduate from the sixth grade, I will be leaving home for the first time to go to school in Salt Lake just like him."

I didn't cry when Sweyn left, but I knew I would bawl like a baby when the day came for Tom to leave.

Our friend Andy Anderson didn't start to school with Tom and me that year. He had stepped on a rusty nail while playing in an abandoned barn on the outskirts of town a couple of weeks before school started. Andy didn't tell his parents about stepping on the rusty nail because he had been forbidden to play in the barn ever since Seth Smith's accident. We had been playing follow-the-leader, and Seth was the leader when the accident happened. Seth was going hand over hand across the rafters in the barn when one of them broke. He had fallen on the railing of a stall, breaking two of his ribs. All the kids in town had been forbidden by their parents to play in the barn after Seth's accident. What parents didn't seem to realize was that this was one sure way to make us kids play in the barn.

Andy knew he would get a whipping if he told his parents about stepping on the rusty nail. He kept the secret of his injured foot from his mother and father until blood poisoning had set in and turned into gangrene. By that time there was nothing else Dr. LeRoy could do but to amputate Andy's left leg just below the knee to prevent the gangrene from spreading. I guess Tom missed Andy more than I did because he was nearer Andy's age, being just a year older.

My first day in school, as I got acquainted with our new teacher, Mr. Standish, I couldn't help thinking that Andy was lucky he didn't have to start to school.

Calvin Whitlock and the other two members of the school board, Mrs. Granger and Mr. Douglas, had decided Miss Thatcher was getting too old to teach school. Without even consulting us kids, they had retired Miss Thatcher and hired Mr. Standish to teach the first through the sixth grades in our one-room schoolhouse. Their decision brought about a complete change in the way students were disciplined. Miss Thatcher had her own system. When a student broke any of the rules, she wrote a note to the parents, leaving the punishment up to the parents. It was a good system because the punishment meted out by the parents was always more drastic than anything Miss Thatcher could have done. Just dipping a girl's pigtails in an inkwell called for a whipping by most parents.

Miss Thatcher had been smart enough to know how tough the first day back at school is for kids. She had always pretended not to see any mischief going on that first day. But Mr. Standish let us know there would be no nonsense even on the first day of school.

He was a man in his late thirties with jet black hair that

118

came to a widow's peak on his forehead, giving him a sinister appearance.

"Students will come to order," he said, rapping a ruler on his desk right after we'd been assigned our desks and seats.

Nobody paid any attention to him because Miss Thatcher had always called us to order three or four times on the first day of school before we obeyed.

Mr. Standish looked at the front row of first graders, then at the second row of second graders, and then at the rows of third, fourth, and fifth graders, and finally at the back row of sixth graders. Not a single student had come to order. Mr. Standish then took out his watch.

"For every minute you fail to come to order," he said, "you will all remain for fifteen minutes after school."

We came to order in a hurry.

Mr. Standish put his watch back in his pocket. Then he pointed at a paddle in the corner. "I am here to educate you children," he said, "and I will not tolerate anything that interferes with your education. The paddle will be used on boys of all ages who shoot spitballs, dip a girl's pigtails in an inkwell, put a frog or any other animal in a girl's desk, throw chalk, or any other infraction of the rules."

Then he picked up a ruler from his desk. "This ruler will be used on the palms of girls who break the rules, and they will be forced to remain after school and clean blackboards and erasers."

Mr. Standish let us know beyond doubt that first day of school, he was not only our teacher but our warden as well. He paddled five boys so hard they all cried. He made three girls remain after school to clean blackboards and erasers.

I was completely cowed when I left the one-room schoolhouse that first day. "That Mr. Standish is a holy terror," I said to Tom as we walked home. "He's got me so scared I'm afraid to go to school."

"He's a mean one all right," Tom agreed.

"I'd hate to be Jimmie Peterson," I said. "Mr. Standish is taking board and room at Jimmie's mother's boarding house. It's tough enough having Mr. Standish for a teacher, but poor old Jimmie has to live in the same house with him."

"I'm not going to worry about Mr. Standish," Tom said.

Three days later Tom had to worry about Mr. Standish. Hal Evans put a live frog in Muriel Cranston's desk. Like any girl, she began screaming and carrying on when she opened her desk and saw the frog. Mr. Standish got the frog and threw it out the window. Then he stood before the class.

"I want the boy who did that to come right up here," he said, which was a silly thing to say in my opinion.

When nobody moved, Mr. Standish pointed at Basil, who had the desk behind Muriel.

"Basil, come up here," Mr. Standish ordered.

This was Basil's first year in an American school. I could tell he was frightened as he stood up.

"I no do it," he said.

"Your desk is right behind Muriel's desk," Mr. Standish said. "If you didn't do it, you must have seen who did."

"I no see," Basil said, so frightened I thought he was going to start jabbering in Greek.

"I think you did," Mr. Standish said. "Now you either tell me who did it if you didn't do it or come up here and take a paddling."

Basil walked to the front of the classroom as Mr. Standish got the paddle from the corner.

120

Tom stood up. "You can't paddle Basil," he said. "He didn't do it."

Mr. Standish looked at Tom like a cat at a mouse. "If you know for a fact that Basil didn't put the frog in Muriel's desk," he said, "then you must know who did. I want the name of the boy who did."

Tom folded his arms on his chest. "I'm no tattletale," he said defiantly.

Mr. Standish told Basil to return to his desk. Then the new teacher ordered Tom to the front of the classroom.

"You will tell me who put the frog in Muriel's desk or take a paddling yourself," Mr. Standish said.

"You can't paddle me for something I didn't do," Tom said, glaring at the teacher.

"But I can paddle you for not telling me who did it." Mr. Standish had an answer for everything.

"I'm not going to tell, and I'm not going to take a paddling," Tom said defiantly.

"We'll see about that," Mr. Standish said as he grabbed my brother and threw Tom across his knees.

I felt tears come into my eyes as I watched Mr. Standish give Tom ten hard whacks with the paddle. The tears weren't for the pain I knew Tom was suffering. I knew my brother could stand pain like an Indian without crying. The tears were for the humiliation I knew Tom was enduring.

"Maybe that will teach you to respect your teacher," Mr. Standish said as he let Tom go.

I was proud of my brother. There were no tears in his eyes as he glared at the new teacher.

"You'll be sorry for this," he said.

Mr. Standish pointed at Tom. "You keep a civil tongue

121

in your head or I'll give you another paddling," he threatened.

It was the rawest deal a kid ever got from a teacher. I couldn't wait for school to let out so we could tell Papa and Uncle Mark. Finally the school day was over and I walked home with my brother.

"When we tell Papa that Mr. Standish paddled you for nothing," I said, "he will write an editorial and get the new teacher fired. And when we tell Uncle Mark, he will arrest Mr. Standish and put the new teacher in jail. There must be some kind of a law against a teacher paddling a kid for nothing."

"We aren't going to tell Papa or Uncle Mark or anybody," Tom said to my surprise. "I can take care of myself. Mr. Standish will rue the day he paddled me because I wouldn't be a tattletale."

My brother sounded like a prophet of doom. I felt a chill come over me.

"What are you going to do?" I asked breathlessly.

"I'm going to put my great brain to work on getting rid of Mr. Standish," Tom answered.

"Oh, boy!" I shouted. "I'd hate to be in his shoes."

"When we get home," Tom said, "I want you to sneak the bottle of liniment out of the medicine cabinet without Mamma seeing you and bring it up to our room. You can rub it on my behind. I'll bet it is black and blue."

I was disappointed when a whole week passed without my brother's great brain devising a scheme for getting rid of Mr. Standish. The new teacher paddled several kids the second week of school. He didn't paddle Tom or me because he had no reason for doing so.

Saturday came. Tom and I did our chores. Then Tom

went up to his loft in the barn to put his great brain to work on getting rid of Mr. Standish. He stayed up in his loft all day.

That night after supper Tom sat on the floor in the parlor, staring into the fireplace. I knew his great brain was working like sixty because his forehead was wrinkled. Just before it was time for our Saturday night baths, he got up and walked over to where Papa was reading the *New York World*.

"What does a schoolteacher have to do to be dismissed by the schoolboard?" he asked.

Papa laid aside the newspaper. "Is Mr. Standish that bad?" he asked. "I know some parents have complained that the new teacher uses the paddle quite freely."

"All the kids hate him and want Miss Thatcher back," Tom said.

"I'm afraid, T.D.," Papa said, "they are going to have to put up with Mr. Standish for at least the rest of the school year. And it is in his contract that he can use the paddle or any other means he wishes to keep discipline in school."

"There must be something a teacher can do that will make a schoolboard dismiss him," Tom said.

"There are several things," Papa said. "A schoolteacher must maintain a reputation that is beyond reproach. Now, a teacher who drank or gambled or used profanity, for example, would be considered too immoral to be in charge of children. But your Mr. Standish does none of these things."

Mamma came into the parlor at that moment and said it was time for our baths. I was the youngest and so I had to go first.

Monday morning during recess I saw Tom talking to Jimmie Peterson. I also saw him hold whispered conversations with several other kids during the afternoon recess. He

124

didn't tell me what was going on until we were on our way home from school that day.

"I've called a meeting in our barn of all the kids who aren't Mormons," he told me.

"Your great brain has figured out a way to get rid of Mr. Standish!" I cried with excitement.

"Mr. Standish will rue the day he paddled me," Tom said.

"But why no Mormon kids?" I asked. "They hate him as much as we do."

"You'll find out why later," Tom said.

A short time later fourteen kids besides Tom and me were assembled in our barn. Tom climbed up the rope ladder to his loft. He came right back down carrying the skull of the Indian chief that always sat on an upturned keg in the loft. He placed it on a bale of hay.

"My great brain has figured out a way to get rid of Mr. Standish," he announced. "But before I tell you about it, I want you all to take an oath on the skull of this dead Indian chief."

Danny Forester had never been up to Tom's loft. "How do we know it is the skull of a dead Indian chief?" he asked.

"Because my Uncle Mark who gave it to me says so,"

125

Tom answered. "He is the marshal and a deputy sheriff and his word is the law. Now do you believe it?"

"If your Uncle Mark says so," Danny answered.

"Now line up," Tom said. "Come forward one at a time and place your right hand on the skull of this dead Indian chief, and swear you will never tell anybody what we are going to do to get rid of Mr. Standish."

One by one we all took the oath never to tell.

Tom then raised his hands over his head. "I call upon the ghost of this dead Indian chief to come back to earth and cut out the tongue of anybody who tells," he chanted. Then he looked at us and said in his natural voice, "And just to make sure, I will personally give two black eyes and a bloody nose to anybody who does tell."

Tom then picked up an empty gunnysack and held it up. "Behold, the first step in Mr. Standish's downfall," he said.

Basil took a step forward. "Me no understand," he said.

"It is only the first step," Tom said. Then he looked at Sammy Leeds. "Can you sneak out of your house after curfew tonight?" he asked.

"Sure," Sammy answered.

"Meet me here," Tom said. "Wait until you hear the curfew whistle blow and then leave your house. The rest of you meet me here tomorrow after school. I will tell you then of the rest of my plan and why no Mormon kids were invited."

I watched Tom remove the screen from our bedroom window that night right after the curfew whistle at the powerhouse sounded. He leaned out the window and grabbed a limb of the elm tree by the side of the house. He went hand over hand down the limb to the trunk of the tree. I watched

126

him shinny down the trunk and disappear into the darkness. I was sure I wouldn't fall asleep until he got back, but the next thing I knew it was morning.

"Did everything go all right last night?" I asked.

"Perfect," Tom answered.

I thought that school day would never end. It just seemed to drag on and on. Tom and I and the other fourteen kids were on our good behavior all day so nobody would be kept after school.

The moment we had been waiting for finally came as we all trooped into our barn after school let out. Tom removed a gunnysack from beneath some hay. Something in it made a tinkling sound.

"Last night under the cover of darkness," Tom said, "Sammy and I, with the stealth of Indian scouts, made our way to the rear of The Whitehorse Saloon. There we obtained part of the evidence that will get rid of Mr. Standish."

I watched breathlessly as Tom removed two empty quart whiskey bottles and two empty pint whiskey flasks from the gunnysack.

"The plan my great brain devised for getting rid of Mr. Standish is to convince the schoolboard that he is a secret drinker," Tom explained. "With Jimmie's help we will plant evidence in Mr. Standish's room."

I thought I saw through the plan. "Jimmie will put the empty whiskey bottles in the teacher's room?"

"Not empty ones," Tom said.

I didn't understand. "How are kids like us going to get whiskey?" I asked.

"My great brain has thought of everything," Tom said confidently. "That is why I didn't let any Mormon kids in on this. The Mormons can't drink whiskey because it's against their religion. Now how many of you have fathers who drink whiskey or keep it in the house for medicinal purposes?"

Twelve kids raised their hands.

"Good," Tom said. "Now how many of you think you could sneak just one drink out of the bottle?"

Basil stepped forward. "Why only one drink?" he asked.

"Because if we take any more our fathers might get suspicious," Tom answered.

"My pa," Danny Forester spoke up, "keeps his bottle in the pantry. I could sneak in there when Ma isn't in the kitchen, but how am I going to carry it?"

"J.D.," Tom said to me, "go up to the loft and get that old hot water bottle of Mamma's."

I scooted up the rope ladder to the loft and back down with the hot water bottle.

"Now watch me closely," Tom said as he took the hot water bottle. "You open your shirt and put the hot water bottle under it and down in your pants. Then you unscrew the top like this." He picked up one of the empty quart whiskey bottles. "Now pretend this is your father's bottle of whiskey. You take the cork out and pour a drink from the whiskey bottle into the hot water bottle. You screw back the cap on the hot water bottle like this. You can button up your shirt and if you hold in your belly you can walk right by anybody without them getting suspicious."

"What a brain!" Danny Forester shouted. "We can go to my house right now. Pa is at work and Ma is over helping my Aunt Sarah do some canning."

"All right, Danny," Tom said with a grin, "we'll begin Mr. Standish's downfall with you."

One of the greatest whiskey raids ever made took place

after school during the rest of the week. Papa's bottle was short a couple of ounces along with the bottles belonging to the fathers of twelve other kids. When the raid was over, there was enough whiskey in the hot water bottle to pour about three ounces of whiskey into each of the pint bottles and about six ounces into one of the quart bottles.

The success of Tom's plan to get rid of Mr. Standish depended a great deal on Jimmie Peterson. Tom met with Jimmie and Sammy Leeds in our barn on Saturday morning. I was permitted to attend the meeting.

"I printed this note," Tom said as he handed Sammy an envelope. "Tomorrow night after curfew you sneak out of your house and slip the note and envelope under Calvin Whitlock's front door. Got it?"

"Got it," Sammy said as he put the note in his pocket.

"Now, Jimmie," Tom said, "tonight after curfew I'll sneak out of the house. I'll hide the pint flask and quart bottle with whiskey in them in your woodshed where I showed you. You've got all day tomorrow to wait for just the perfect chance to sneak them up to your room and hide them. Monday morning after Mr. Standish leaves for the school-house, it will be up to you to hide the pint flask under his pillow and the quart bottle in his clothes closet. Got it?"

"Got it," Jimmie said, grinning.

"Tomorrow night after curfew," Tom said, "I'll sneak out of the house again and put the empty quart bottle in Mrs. Taylor's trash can where she will be sure to see it Monday morning when she goes to the backhouse. And I'll plant the other pint flask with whiskey in it in Mr. Standish's coat pocket at school Monday morning."

Everything went without a hitch that weekend, and on Monday morning Tom's plan for getting rid of the new teacher went into action. Jimmie was in the kitchen where his mother was preparing breakfast for her boarders when Mrs. Taylor knocked on the back door. Jimmie's mother opened the door.

"I'll thank you, Mrs. Peterson," Mrs. Taylor said as she waved the empty quart whiskey bottle that Tom had planted in her trash can, "to tell your boarders that I do not want them throwing their empty whiskey bottles in my trash can."

"So, it is Mrs. Peterson instead of Jenny is it?" Jimmie's mother said. "Well, I'll thank you, Mrs. Taylor, not to be accusing my boarders of doing such a thing. None of my boarders ever touches a drop."

"Where else could this bottle have come from?" Mrs. Taylor demanded. "You and your boarders are the only people in the block who aren't Mormons, and you know us Mormons never touch alcohol."

"Then you must have a backslider in your midst," Jimmie's mother said. "I would not take in a boarder who drank or smoked."

And with that, Jimmie told us later, his mother slammed the door in Mrs. Taylor's face.

After eating breakfast, Jimmie waited in his room until he saw Mr. Standish leave for the schoolhouse. Then he slipped into the teacher's room and put the pint flask under the pillow and hid the quart bottle in the clothes closet. And for an added touch that Tom had thought up on Sunday, Jimmie placed an open package of Sen Sen, which had cost my brother five cents, on the teacher's dresser.

Mr. Standish kept a black alpaca coat at the schoolhouse, which he wore during school hours. He hung his regular coat in the hallway on one of the hooks used by pupils. It was no trick at all for Tom to sneak into the hallway that Monday

morning and plant the pint flask in the teacher's inside coat pocket.

What followed I didn't learn until later, but I'm going to tell it as it happened.

Calvin Whitlock had his breakfast interrupted that morning by his housekeeper, Mrs. Hazzelton, who handed him the note Sammy had slipped under the front door. It read:

THE NEW SCHOOLTEACHER IS A SECRET DRINKER. IF YOU DON'T BELIEVE IT, LOOK IN HIS COAT POCKET AT SCHOOL AND SEARCH HIS ROOM.

Mr. Whitlock immediately telephoned the other two schoolboard members. The three of them went to Mrs. Peterson's boarding house. They arrived just as Jimmie's mother was coming out of the house.

131

"I was just on my way to see you," she said to Mr. Whitlock. "I will not tolerate any drinkers in my boarding house. And I certainly will not tolerate any teacher who drinks as a teacher for my son, Jimmie."

"You discovered this only now?" Mr. Whitlock asked.

"Just this morning," Mrs. Peterson replied.

"Then you didn't write the note?" Mr. Whitlock asked.

"What note?" Mrs. Peterson asked.

The banker showed Jimmie's mother the note.

"It's printed," Mrs. Peterson said, "but I wouldn't be surprised if it wasn't Mrs. Taylor who wrote it. It all started with her coming to the house this morning and accusing one of my boarders of throwing empty whiskey bottles in her trash can. I couldn't believe it was one of my boarders until I went up to make up Mr. Standish's room. Laying right under his pillow where he'd forgotten it was a pint bottle with whiskey in it. And on his dresser there was an open package of Sen Sen which he took to kill the odor of the whiskey on his breath."

"Did you leave the bottle where you found it?" Mr. Whitlock asked.

When Mrs. Peterson nodded, the banker said he would need the bottle for evidence. They all went up to the teacher's room.

"I never did like that man," Mrs. Granger said as they entered the room. "There was something about him I just didn't like."

Mr. Whitlock removed the pint flask from under the pillow and put it in his pocket. Then he looked around the room. "With a man like this you never know," he said. "Perhaps we should search the room."

When the quart bottle with whiskey in it was found in

132

the clothes closet, Mr. Whitlock exclaimed with disgust, "The man is nothing but a drunken sot. Whiskey under his pillow. Whiskey in his clothes closet. And according to the note he even takes whiskey to school with him. How could we have been so taken in by such a man?"

The two bottles and the package of Sen Sen were placed in a brown paper bag. Mr. Whitlock was carrying the paper bag when he and the other two members of the schoolboard entered the schoolhouse. They went directly into the hallway where they found the pint flask with whiskey in it in the teacher's coat pocket. This bottle joined the others in the brown paper bag. Then Mr. Whitlock and the two board members came into the classroom. The banker's face was red with anger as he looked at Mr. Standish.

"You will dismiss school for today immediately," Mr. Whitlock said, "and report to me and the other board members at my home this afternoon at two o'clock sharp."

Tom was rubbing his hands gleefully as we left the schoolhouse. "I told you I would make Mr. Standish rue the day he paddled me," he chuckled. "He was a fool to go up against my great brain."

Papa was upset when he came home for lunch. "I met Calvin Whitlock this morning," he told Mamma. "The schoolboard is meeting this afternoon to dismiss Mr. Standish."

"Because of the paddlings?" Mamma asked.

"No," Papa said, shaking his head, "it seems that Mr. Standish is a secret drinker."

"I can't believe it," Mamma said.

"Calvin has more than enough evidence to prove it," Papa said. "He told me they would rehire Miss Thatcher until such a time as they can get another teacher."

"Hurray!" Tom shouted.

Papa gave Tom a funny look. Then he shook his head as if dismissing some crazy idea he might have had.

When Papa came home for supper that night, he was very quiet. He hardly spoke at all until Mamma and Aunt Bertha had finished the supper dishes and came into the parlor. Mamma looked at him as she sat down in her maple rocker.

"What is on your mind?" she asked.

"I can't get Mr. Standish off my mind," Papa said. "The poor man came to see me this afternoon after being dismissed by the schoolboard. He swears he never took a drink in his life and doesn't know how the whiskey got into his room or in his coat pocket at school."

"Isn't that about what a secret drinker who was a schoolteacher would say?" Mamma asked.

"I suppose so," Papa said, "but I flatter myself I am a pretty good judge of character. I just can't believe Mr. Standish is guilty. The man swore before God to me that he was innocent and somebody must have framed him." Papa shrugged helplessly. "But who in the world would do a contemptible thing like that?"

Tom got up from the floor where we were playing dominoes. He walked over to Papa.

"Why did you say 'contemptible'?" he asked.

"What would you call a person who ruined my reputation with false evidence?" Papa said.

"But that is different," Tom said. "Every kid in school hates Mr. Standish."

"That is no excuse," Papa said. "If Mr. Standish is innocent, as he claims to be, somebody in this town has done one of the cruelest things one man can do to another." Papa turned his head and looked at Mamma. "Mrs. Peterson wouldn't even let the poor man in the house. She had his things packed and placed on the front porch. He had to take a room at the Sheepmen's Hotel. He is leaving for Salt Lake City in the morning. I can't help feeling sorry for him, guilty or innocent."

"But, Papa," Tom protested, "Mr. Standish paddled me because I wouldn't be a tattletale. He had no right to paddle me for that."

I thought Papa was going to choke. His face turned red and his cheeks puffed up like a tormented bullfrog. Then he relaxed.

"It couldn't be," he said as if reassuring himself. "The whiskey rules it out."

Mamma knew my brother better than Papa did. She crooked her finger and motioned to Tom with a stern look on her face. Tom walked over and stood in front of her.

"Tom Dennis," Mamma said sharply, "I have a sneaking suspicion that you know something. If you do know anything that will prove Mr. Standish innocent of these charges, you had better speak up right now."

"He had no right to paddle me." Tom said stubbornly.

"But the whiskey . . ." Papa cried out as if in pain.

I jumped to my feet. "Twelve kids helped us get it," I said without thinking.

"Oh, no!" Papa said with a groan as he pressed the palms of his hands to the sides of his head.

"Tom's great brain figured out how to get rid of the new teacher," I said, thinking now that I'd spilled the beans I might as well spill some more.

Papa's mouth flapped open and shut without any words coming from it as he looked helplessly at Mamma. For the first time in my life I saw Mamma so stunned she couldn't react quickly to a crisis as she stared at me with her mouth open. I couldn't help but feel a little proud of myself at making both my parents speechless.

Papa finally recovered his voice. "Son," he said to Tom, "to ruin a man's good name is about as low and mean a thing as one person can do to another. If you can save Mr. Standish's reputation and refuse to speak, your mother and I will never forgive you."

"I swore I'd never tell," Tom said. Then he gave me a dirty look. "And so did J.D."

"There comes a time in every man's life," Papa said, "when he must break his word to help somebody."

"But you always said that a man's word was his bond," Tom argued.

Papa looked helplessly at Mamma who was fully recovered now.

"We will have no more of this nonsense, Tom Dennis," Mamma said sternly. "A man's entire future is at stake. You will tell your father and me exactly what happened right from the beginning."

Tom hesitated for a moment, then said, "All right, I'll tell."

I watched the expression on Papa's face change from interest to surprise and then to astonishment and finally to complete unadulterated awe as Tom confessed.

"I told Mr. Standish he would be sorry for paddling me," Tom said in conclusion. "He was a fool to think he could go up against my great brain and win."

"I have never laid a hand on you," Papa said, breathing heavily, "but right at this moment if I had that paddle, I'm afraid I would give you a paddling that would make the one you got from Mr. Standish seem like patty-cakes,"

Then Papa stood up and got very dramatic as he looked at Mamma. "So help me, Tena," he said, "if the stars stop shining some night and the sun fails to come up some morning, I will know who to blame. Calvin Whitlock is going to have to call another schoolboard meeting tonight at his home." Then he pointed at Tom. "And you are going to be the star witness," Papa said emphatically.

"Can I be a witness too?" I asked, not wanting to be left out of things.

"I think," Papa said, "that admitting one Fitzgerald was the ring leader in all of this is about all I can stand for one evening."

Mamma let me stay up that night until Papa and Tom returned from the schoolboard meeting. Tom told me about the meeting as we got undressed for bed. He said he had confessed everything except one thing.

"I didn't tattle on any of the kids who were in on it," he told me. "They knew Jimmie Peterson must have been in on it but I didn't say so."

It was strange but I never thought about the oath I'd taken on the skull of the dead Indian chief until I tried to go to sleep that night. Everytime I closed my eyes I would see the ghost of the dead Indian chief sneaking into the room with a knife to cut my tongue out. I began to cry.

"What's eating you, J.D.?" Tom asked, sitting up in bed.

I told him. He began to laugh.

"It isn't funny," I said.

"Shucks, J.D.," Tom said. "There is no such thing as a ghost."

137

"But you told all the kids—"

"That was just to throw a scare into them," Tom interrupted me. "Now if there were such things as ghosts, don't you think my great brain would know it?"

"Sure," I said.

"Well, my great brain knows there is no such thing as a ghost," Tom said, "so go to sleep and forget about it."

I was almost asleep when Tom said, "I'm sorry in a way there are no ghosts. If there were I'd put my great brain to work on how to communicate with them."

The next morning Mr. Standish rapped his ruler on his desk to bring the students to order. I figured his first business of the day would be to give Tom at least twenty whacks with the paddle. I was dead wrong.

"I have something to say to one boy in this room," Mr. Standish said. "I didn't have an opportunity to thank that boy last night. Regardless of what that boy did to me, he more than made up for it with his courage and kindness in coming to my defense. That particular boy has made it possible for me to go on doing the thing I love the most—teaching. To show my appreciation, we will revert to the system Miss Thatcher used. When any student breaks the rules, that student will be given a note to take home. The punishment for the infraction of rules will be left to the parents."

Well, it was like Papa said to Mamma when they imposed a whole week of the silent treatment as punishment for me and Tom.

"T.D. will probably come out of this a hero to every kid in school," Papa said, and that is just how it turned out.

CHAPTER EIGHT

The Great Brain's Reformation

IT WAS THE FIRST WEEK in November before Andy Anderson was able to attend school. Mr. Jamison, the carpenter, had built a wooden peg leg for Andy with a pad made from leather where the knee rested.

At first all of us kids were quite awed by the peg leg. We tried it on and walked on it. But the novelty soon wore off and we began calling him Peg Leg. Andy couldn't join us in most of the games we played. His father must have realized this and had ordered an erector set from Sears Roebuck. I guess he thought the erector set would draw kids to the Anderson home where they would play with Andy. He was right. I learned from Howard Kay one Saturday morning

139

that the erector set had arrived. We ran all the way to the Anderson home.

Andy came hobbling on his peg leg to the front door after we had rung the bell. Howard and I reminded him we were his friends. He invited us into the house and we played with the erector set until noon.

I told Tom about it as we sat on the front porch waiting for Mamma to call us for lunch.

"Gosh, T.D.," I said, still filled with wonder, "you never saw anything like it in your life. You can build windmills, steam shovels, cranes, and all kinds of things that actually work when you turn a crank."

"I saw the picture of the set in the Sears Roebuck catalog," Tom said. "It costs six dollars. If I had a set like that, I could make a fortune."

"How?" I asked.

"By charging kids a penny an hour to play with it," Tom answered. Then his face became thoughtful. "Maybe I can work out a deal with Andy."

"No, you can't," I said. "His father bought him the set so kids would play with Andy. You start charging and some kid will tell Andy's father."

"I guess you're right," Tom admitted. "To heck with the erector set. After lunch we will go to the Jensen place and get your pup. They have been weaned now for over three weeks and are just about right to take home."

After lunch Tom told me to take Brownie with us.

"Lady won't make any fuss about losing her pups if she thinks they are going with their father," Tom said wisely.

Frank and Allan Jensen were waiting in the backyard by Lady's doghouse. Brownie ran around smelling the pups and playing with them. Then he sat on his haunches, looking proud as all get out.

Lady had given birth to five male puppies and three females. Tom picked up the male pups one at a time and carefully examined them. He took his time before handing me one of the male pups.

"This is the best of the litter," Tom said.

I held the puppy so he could lick my face and get to know me.

"Take your second pick," Allan said to Tom.

I looked at Allan. "Are you going to give T.D. a pup for rescuing you from Skeleton Cave?" I asked.

"Shucks, no," Allan said. "You can't pay anybody for saving your life. This is part of the deal we made with Tom before we got lost in the cave."

"What deal?" I asked, and couldn't help feeling I was somehow getting swindled.

"Tom wouldn't let us mate Lady with Brownie until we promised him the pick of the litter for you and a male pup for him," Allan explained.

Well, I should have known there had to be a catch in it when Tom had so generously offered to help me get the best pup for nothing.

Tom made his selection. He cradled the male pup in his arm. "You're sure they have been weaned for at least three weeks?" he asked Frank.

Frank nodded. "Just like Mr. Monaire said."

I knew Mr. Monaire was the biggest sheepman in the county. I couldn't understand what business it was of his. I looked at Frank and Allan.

"Are you going to give Mr. Monaire the extra pups?"

141

I asked, knowing the owner of a female dog usually kept only one or two pups out of a litter.

They both looked at Tom, who answered me. "Mr. Monaire wanted the pups he is going to buy to be old enough to send out with his sheepherders," he said.

"Going to buy?" I asked with astonishment. In all my life I'd never heard of anybody paying for a pup.

"These aren't ordinary pups," Tom said. "They will make excellent sheep dogs. Mr. Monaire promised to pay two dollars for each male and one dollar for each female." Then he looked at Frank and Allan. "How many are you going to sell?" he asked.

Frank shrugged. "We can only sell two of the females," he said. "Pa promised neighbors two male pups and one female. He said we could keep just one male pup."

Allan picked up two of the female puppies as Lady began to whine.

I followed them, with Brownie tagging along at my heels, down to the stockyards by the railroad tracks. There were hundreds of sheep in the stock pens. Sheepherders with sheep dogs were busy separating the sheep being sent to market from the ones to be turned out for winter grazing. Mr. Monaire was standing by the shearing pens.

"Here are the pups by Brownie and Lady like I promised last spring," Tom said to Mr. Monaire. "This one is a male. Frank and Allan have two females they want to sell."

Mr. Monaire carefully examined the three pups. "They will make fine sheep dogs," he said. Then he called to a sheepherder and told the man to take the pups.

I watched bug-eyed as Mr. Monaire took out his purse

and handed Tom two silver dollars and Frank and Allan a silver dollar apiece.

Mr. Monaire patted the head of the pup in my arms. "Want to sell your pup, son?" he asked. "I promise we'll take good care of him."

"No, sir," I said.

We left the stockyards with Tom jingling the two silver dollars in his pocket and Frank and Allan flipping their dollars into the air and catching them. I was so full of indignation I thought I'd bust wide open. I wanted to denounce my brother as a swindler and cheat on the spot. But I'd made a promise to Mamma one time that I would never argue with my brothers in front of other kids. I waited until we got to Main Street and Frank and Allan turned off to go home.

"You cheated me!" I cried.

Tom stopped and stared at me as if I'd suddenly turned into a horned toad.

"How can you say a thing like that?" he asked with indignation. "You got the pick of the litter didn't you?"

"But you got two dollars," I accused him.

"You can sell your pup for two dollars too," Tom said.

"I don't want to sell my pup," I cried.

"Then what are you griping about?" Tom demanded.

"I think I got cheated," I said.

Tom put his hand on my shoulder. "Now listen to me, J.D.," he said earnestly. "Last spring when I saw Brownie making up to a female dog for the first time, I put my great brain to work. I took Brownie and Lady to see Mr. Monaire. I told him that Brownie was a purebred Alaskan and Lady was a genuine sheep dog. He carefully examined both dogs and agreed with me. I then drove a hard bargain with Mr. Mon-

aire. I got him to agree to pay two dollars for any male pup and one dollar for any female pup by Lady and Brownie."

"So what?" I asked. "I still say you cheated me."

"Now, let us assume," Tom said, "that I hadn't put my great brain to work last spring. What would have happened? We would have mated Brownie with Lady. Right?"

"Right," I said.

"And Lady would have had her litter of pups. Right?"

"Right," I agreed.

"And as the owner of the male dog you would have been entitled to the pick of the litter. Right?"

"Right," I said.

"And the pup you now hold in your arms is the pick of the litter. Right?"

"Right," I said.

"Then how can you possibly say I cheated you?" Tom asked as if I'd hurt his feelings terribly.

"I don't know," I said all confused, "but it still doesn't seem right to me."

"But you just agreed with me that everything I said was right, J.D., and how can so many rights be wrong?"

"I know I did but . . ." I couldn't finish the sentence because I couldn't think of anything to put after the but.

"You know the Jensens are not rich," Tom said.

"Sure," I admitted, "but what has that got to do with it?"

"Frank and Allan never had a whole dollar of their own in their lives," Tom said. "If it hadn't been for me and my great brain, their father would have given the extra pups away. Are you so selfish and jealous, J.D., that you wouldn't want poor Frank and Allan to ever have a dollar of their own?"

"Gosh, no," I said.

145

"Well, you are certainly acting like it," Tom said.

"I am?" I asked.

"You certainly are," Tom said.

I felt ashamed. "I didn't mean to," I said, trying to defend myself.

"And to top it off," Tom said, looking really hurt now, "you accuse me, your own brother, of cheating you. I was only looking out for your interest all the time. I wanted to be sure you got the best male pup of the litter and you did. To show you my heart is in the right place, J.D., I'm going to treat you to a nickel's worth of candy at the Z.C.M.I. store."

Such generosity made me feel even more ashamed. "I'm sorry I said you cheated me," I apologized.

We walked over to the Z.C.M.I. store, and not until I was munching on a stick of licorice did my brother speak to me again.

"I accept the apology you made a while ago on one condition," he said.

Eating licorice purchased by and given to me by my brother, I was in no position to argue. But I did think I was at least entitled to know what the condition was.

"What condition?" I asked.

"That you don't tell Mamma and Papa about the deal I made with Mr. Monaire," Tom said. "When my great brain rescued Frank and Allan from Skeleton Cave, it made me quite a hero in Mamma's and Papa's eyes. I wouldn't want them thinking the deal I made with Mr. Monaire had anything to do with it. I would have put my great brain to work to rescue Frank and Allan even if Lady hadn't been with them."

I couldn't remember exactly at the moment, but it

seemed to me Tom hadn't put his great brain to work on the rescue until after he'd told me it would cost him a fortune if Frank and Allan weren't rescued. I couldn't bite the hand that was feeding me licorice at the moment, so I gave my brother the benefit of the doubt. And yet . . .

I didn't realize how cruel we kids were to Andy Anderson until the following Saturday. Tom and I were playing marbles with Andy in our backyard. It was one of the few games Andy could still play. Sammy Leeds, Basil, Jimmie Peterson, Danny Forester, and Howard Kay came into the yard from the alley.

"We're going to play Kick the Can," Sammy said. "Want to play?"

"Sure," I said, jumping to my feet.

Tom picked up his marbles and shoved them into his pocket. He got to his feet. "Let's go," he said.

We all ran into the alley except Andy. Tom drew a line in the dirt. We stood twenty feet away and tossed rocks at the line. Sammy's rock landed farthest from the line. He was "it." The rest of us ran to hide as Sammy set up a tin can in the alley. The purpose of the game was to kick the can without letting Sammy tag us. If he did tag one of us before we kicked the can, then whoever he tagged had to be "it." Tom ran into the alley, pretending he was going to kick the can, just to get Sammy to chase him. Basil sneaked behind Sammy and kicked the can. Sammy had to get the can and put it back in place.

We had been playing for some time and Basil was "it" when I decided to sneak into our woodshed. I could watch through a crack until Basil got far enough away from the can for me to run out of the woodshed and kick it. I entered the woodshed.

147

Andy was sitting on the chopping block with his back toward me. He was crying.

"Darn old peg leg," he sobbed. "Darn no good old peg leg. I wish I was dead."

I crept back out of the woodshed without letting him know I'd seen and heard.

The following Saturday afternoon Tom and I were on our front lawn playing at Indian wrestling with Andy watching us. Sammy and the gang came along on their way to the Smiths' vacant lot to play One-O-Cat ball. Sammy had his ball and bat with him. Tom and I ran into the house to get our mitts.

Just as we came out the front door with our mitts, I saw Andy going around the corner of our house. I tossed my mitt on the front porch swing and followed him. I saw Andy walk around to the rear of our barn. I crept closer. Andy was sitting with his back against the barn. He had his arms around his knees, with his head buried on them. His shoulders were shaking. He was crying so hard it looked as if his whole body was trembling.

I didn't want him to know I'd been spying on him. I crept around to the front of the barn. I made a lot of noise entering it. Then I pushed the loose board aside at the rear and stepped out.

Andy was wiping his eyes with his sleeve. "I thought you went to play ball," he said as if he resented me being there.

"I changed my mind," I said as I sat down beside him.

"Because you feel sorry for me," he said with bitterness in his voice.

"Sure I feel sorry for you," I said. "But is it really so bad having a peg leg?"

148

"What good is a kid with a peg leg?" he asked hopelessly. "I can't run and play with the other kids. I can't do my chores. It's like my Pa said. I'm plumb useless."

"Your father said you were plumb useless?" I asked, unable to believe any father could be so cruel.

"He didn't know I heard him," Andy said. "I tried doing my chores for the first time when I got home from school yesterday. I got an armful of kindling from the woodshed. I fell trying to get up the back porch steps and spilled it. Then I dropped and spilled a bucket of coal. Then I tried to collect the eggs in the hen house and I dropped and broke them. Then Ma told me not to try to do any chores anymore. And when Pa came home, she told him. Pa didn't know I was on the back porch and could hear him and Ma in the kitchen. That was when he said they would have to take care of me the rest of my life because I was plumb useless."

"I guess that makes you plumb useless all right," I said.

"What's the use of me going on living when I'm plumb useless?" Andy asked.

"Not much," I said, thinking how it would be if I couldn't play with other kids and my own father thought I was plumb useless.

"I'm going to do myself in," Andy said desperately.

I couldn't help getting excited. "You mean you are going to kill yourself?" I cried.

"Give me one good reason why not," Andy said.

I thought and I thought and I thought but I couldn't think of one good reason. I was about ready to give up when I thought of the erector set.

"You are the only kid in town with an erector set," I said, hoping that would cheer him up.

149

"What good is an erector set when I'm plumb useless like my pa said?" Andy asked. Then he looked at me. "Will you help me, John?"

I couldn't turn down a friend in need. "Sure," I promised.

"We've got to figure out a way to do myself in good and proper," Andy said with a serious expression.

We discussed several ways for Andy to kill himself, only to discard them. I had never realized before what a problem it was for a person to figure out a way to kill himself. I was about to suggest we get Tom and his great brain to figure it out for us when Andy came up with an idea that sounded promising.

"When people want to get rid of kittens they don't want," he said, "they put them in a gunnysack and throw them into the river."

"That is a good idea," I admitted, "but I'm not strong enough to carry you in a gunnysack down to the river and throw you in."

"You don't have to carry me down there," Andy said.

"You mean I'll tie you up in the sack when we get there?" I asked.

"You'll have to tie the sack good and hard so I can't get out," Andy said, "because I'm a good swimmer, peg leg and all."

I was by this time quite excited and enthusiastic about the plan. "I'll tie you in the sack and roll you off the diving board into the deepest part of the swimming hole," I said. Then I looked up at the snow on the mountain peaks. "But that water in the river is going to be mighty cold," I warned him.

150

"Who cares how cold the water is when I'm going to drown?" Andy asked. "Let's go."

We went into the barn. I got a big gunnysack that was empty. It was the kind oats came in to feed to our team of horses and Sweyn's mustang, Dusty. It was plenty big enough for drowning Andy. Then I got some twine. We started out for the river. Andy was very happy and cheerful at the prospect of doing himself in. It made me feel good knowing I was helping to make him happy and cheerful.

When we arrived at the swimming hole, Andy took off his peg leg and stripped down to his underwear.

"Maybe my folks will have another son someday who can wear my clothes," he said as his body began shivering from the cold wind blowing off the mountains. "See that they get them. I'm giving my peg leg to you, John."

"What will I do with it?" I asked.

"I don't know," he said. "I just thought you might like it to sort of remember me."

"That would be nice," I had to admit.

I helped Andy get into the gunnysack. I closed the top of it and tied it with twine. Then I rolled him in the gunnysack to the riverbank. I located his head in the sack and patted it.

"We are at the diving board," I told him. "I'm going to roll you up the diving board now. You can sort of help by turning yourself as I push you."

I was afraid Andy would fall off the diving board before we reached the end of it, but he didn't. Again I patted him on the head.

"One more push and you are a goner," I said. "Are you ready, old pal?"

151

"Tell my folks I did it because I'm plumb useless."
Andy's voice came out of the gunnysack. "And I sure appreciate you helping me to do myself in. You are a real pal, John. I'm ready."

"Good-bye, old pal," I said, feeling very sad as I rolled Andy off the end of the diving board.

The gunnysack with Andy in it hit the water. I was expecting to see a few air bubbles after the big splash as Andy went to his death. Instead the water began to churn and to my astonishment Andy's head popped out of it. He began swimming toward the river bank as the gunnysack floated down the river. I ran to meet him.

"Gee whizz, John," he said with his teeth chattering from the cold water, "couldn't you tie a knot that would hold? The sack busted right open when I hit the water."

I was a little nettled by his attitude. I thought I'd tied a good knot. "You could have pretended the sack didn't open and let yourself drown," I pointed out to him.

"Even a fool knows when you know how to swim you can't let yourself drown," he said as if completely disgusted with me.

"I'll run back to the barn and get another sack and some baling wire," I said. "I'll tie you in with baling wire so you'll never get out."

"It is too darn cold," Andy said as he started to dress with his clothes sticking to his wet body. "Let's figure out a better way."

"Maybe you'll get pneumonia and die," I said, trying to cheer him up.

"I ain't that lucky," he said.

We were both pretty disgusted when we returned to the barn. Andy was disgusted because he was still alive. I was disgusted because I'd let a pal down. We sat down at the rear of the barn in the sun so Andy's clothes would dry.

"I guess we'll have to get Tom to help us," I said. "With his great brain he could figure out a dozen ways to put you out of your misery."

"No, John," Andy said. "Tom might decide to tell my folks instead. It is up to you and me. I know I can trust you."

I saw a broken bottle lying in the weeds. "How about slashing your wrists with that broken bottle and letting yourself bleed to death right here?" I suggested.

Andy thought about it for a moment. "That is too messy," he finally said.

We sat there until Andy's clothes were all dry, trying to think of a way for him to commit suicide. I was about to give up when I heard Sweyn's mustang, Dusty, moving around in his stall inside the barn. It reminded me of how they hang outlaws.

"I've got it!" I cried with excitement. "How about hanging you? That isn't messy."

Andy's face broke into a grin. "That is a peach of an idea," he said.

"We'll hang you just like they hang outlaws," I said.

"But I'm no outlaw," Andy protested.

"You can pretend you are one can't you?" I asked.

"Why must I pretend to be an outlaw?" Andy wanted to know.

"Look, Andy," I said a little exasperated with him, "I promised Sweyn when he went to Salt Lake to school that I would take good care of Dusty. You don't think I'd let Dusty hang anybody who wasn't an outlaw, do you? It wouldn't be fair to Dusty. He's got to think he is hanging a sure enough outlaw."

153

"All right," Andy agreed. "I'll pretend I'm an outlaw for Dusty's sake."

We went into the barn. I got Sweyn's lariat and climbed up the rope ladder to Tom's loft. I tossed one end of the lariat over a rafter and let the rope slide down until Andy got a hold of it. I climbed down the rope ladder. I tied a slipknot noose on one end of the lariat. I was still a little angry about Andy bawling me out for the knot I'd tied on the gunnysack. I handed the rope to him.

"Are you satisfied that is a good strong noose that won't come loose?" I asked.

Andy inspected the noose very carefully. "I'm satisfied," he said.

I put a halter on Dusty and led the mustang out of his stall to the side of a bale of hay. I helped Andy onto the bale of hay and from there to Dusty's back. I got some twine and stood on the bale of hay while I tied Andy's hands behind his back. Then I put the noose over Andy's head and pulled the slipknot until the noose was tight around his neck. I jumped down from the bale of hay and got the other end of the lariat. I tied it securely to a stall post. I stood back and looked at the lariat from the stall post to the rafter and back down to Andy's neck. It was tight. All was in readiness for the hanging.

"Dusty," I said to the mustang, "that isn't Andy Anderson on your back. That is the no good outlaw Peg Leg Andy you are about to hang."

Dusty looked at me as if he understood. I walked around behind him.

"Are you ready to hang, you no good outlaw?" I asked Andy.

"Ready," Andy replied. "And before I go, John, I want

you to know how much I appreciate you helping me to do myself in. You are a real pal."

I took off my cap and raised my arm. I hit Dusty over the rump with my cap. I expected the mustang to jump and leave Andy dangling from the end of the lariat. Dusty didn't move. I hit him again with my cap and let out an Indian war cry at the same time. Dusty turned his head and looked at me with his ears flattened back, which meant he was angry. I hit him again with my cap and let out a real blood-curdling Indian war cry.

Dusty turned slowly around so Andy wouldn't fall off. He grabbed my cap out of my hand with his teeth. He dropped the cap by his forelegs and put a hoof on it. Then he twisted his head and rubbed his nose against Andy's good leg.

"He knows you because Sweyn let you ride him a few times," I said. "He knows you aren't an outlaw."

"See if you can lead him," Andy said. "I ain't got all day."

I took hold of the halter. I pulled on it. I begged Dusty to move. I coaxed him. I threatened him. All Dusty did was to flatten his ears back to let me know he was plenty angry at me.

"Try kicking him in the flanks," I said to Andy.

Andy kicked Dusty in the flanks. At any other time Dusty would have bucked like crazy. But he didn't move an inch. His ears got flatter and flatter as Andy kicked him in the flanks and I pulled on the halter.

"What the devil is going on here?" I heard Tom's voice behind me.

"I'm trying to hang an outlaw," I said over my shoulder, "but Dusty won't help me."

"Stop it, you fool!" Tom shouted. "You could kill Andy."

"That is the idea," I said as I continued to pull on the halter and Andy kept on kicking Dusty in the flanks. "Andy is plumb useless with his peg leg and wants to do himself in. I'm his pal and I'm helping him."

Tom grabbed the halter out of my hands. "Steady, boy," he said to Dusty as he patted the mustang on the nose. "Now, J.D.," he said to me as he kept patting Dusty on the nose, "untie the lariat from the stall post."

I knew Dusty wasn't going to cooperate so I untied the lariat.

Tom let go of the halter. He took out his jackknife and stepped on top of the bale of hay. He cut the twine I'd used to tie Andy's wrists. Then he loosened the noose and slipped the lariat over Andy's head. He then helped Andy down from the mustang. If he was expecting any thanks, he sure got a surprise.

"Why did you have to butt in?" Andy asked as tears came into his eyes.

Tom looked surprised all right. "You mean you actually wanted to commit suicide and weren't just playing a game?" he asked, looking astonished.

"What good is a kid with a peg leg?" Andy sobbed as he sat down on the bale of hay and put his face in his hands. "I can't play with the other kids. I can't do my chores. I'm just plumb useless like Pa said and better off dead."

"Nobody is plumb useless," Tom said.

"A lot you know," Andy cried. "Even with your great brain you can't grow me another leg."

"Of course I can't," Tom admitted. "But my great brain can prove to the world that you aren't plumb useless."

156

For the first time since Andy had lost his leg, I saw hope come into his eyes as he looked at Tom. "If you can prove I'm not plumb useless to my pa, I'll give you anything I've got," he promised.

A cunning look spread over Tom's face. "Even your erector set?" he asked.

Andy hesitated. "I don't know if Pa would let me," he said.

"What would your pa do with the erector set if you committed suicide?" Tom asked. "If you want to commit suicide or go on being plumb useless over an erector set, that is your business." Tom started for the barn door.

"Wait. Tom!" Andy shouted. "It's a deal."

Tom turned around and walked over to the bale of hay. He held out his hand. "Let's shake on it," he said.

They shook hands to seal the bargain.

"I'll put my great brain to work on it right away," Tom promised Andy. "Meet me here after school starting Monday."

After Andy left the barn to go home, Tom began to rub his hands together gleefully. "I'll make a fortune with that erector set, charging kids a penny an hour to play with it," he said.

That evening after supper Tom sat staring into the burning log in the fireplace in our parlor for a long time before he got up and walked over to Papa.

"Papa," he said, "is it true that when a person loses an arm or a leg, they get twice the strength in the other arm or leg?"

Papa laid aside a book he was reading. "Perhaps not twice the strength, T.D.," he said, "but I have heard it said on good authority that a person does have more strength in

157

the remaining limb. One theory is that it is a biological thing, and when a human body loses a limb, an organic change takes place which transfers more strength to the remaining limb. Another theory, and a much more logical one, is that when a person loses an arm or a leg, he will naturally use the remaining limb a great deal more, and this would of course strengthen that limb. I did know a one-armed miner in Silverlode who had twice the strength of a normal man in his one arm. I saw him perform feats of strength with that one arm that were amazing."

"Thank you, Papa," Tom said, smiling.

Tom and I were waiting in our barn Monday after school when Andy arrived. Tom put his hands on Andy's shoulders.

"Do you promise to put yourself in complete charge of my great brain and do everything I tell you to do?" he asked.

"I promise," Andy said.

"Good," Tom said. "The first thing you've got to do is to stop feeling sorry for yourself."

"I'll betcha you'd feel sorry for yourself if you had a peg leg," Andy said.

"No, I wouldn't," Tom said to my surprise, "because I'd show every kid in town and my mother and my father that a peg leg didn't make any difference. We will start by making you the best Indian squaw wrestler in town."

"Fat chance," Andy said. "Basil is the champion."

"Now you listen to me, Andy Anderson," Tom said, getting angry. "When a person loses one leg, he gets twice the strength in the remaining leg. That means you've got double the strength in your right leg of any kid your age and size in town. My papa is the smartest man in town and he said this was true. Are you calling my father a liar?"

"Gosh, no," Andy said quickly. "My pa always said that your pa was the smartest man in town."

"Then you must believe you've got twice the strength in your right leg than you would have if you had two legs," Tom said. "And that means you should be able to beat any kids at Indian squaw wrestling who are bigger and older than you."

Tom got a horse blanket from Dusty's stall. He spread it out on the floor of the barn. He lay down on his back. He motioned for Andy to lay down beside him with their feet at each other's head. They locked their right arms at the elbow. Tom began to count. They raised their right legs at the count of one and let them down. At the count of two they again raised their right legs and let them down. At the count of three they locked their right legs at the knees. The winner in Indian squaw wrestling was the one who could force an opponent's leg down, and keel the opponent over backward in a somersault.

I watched breathlessly as they both began to grunt. Tom slowly forced Andy's leg down and Andy went over backward.

Tom sat up on the horse blanket. He looked sternly at Andy. "Papa says you've got twice the strength in your right leg of any kid in town your age," he said.

That wasn't what Papa had said at all, but I knew it was part of The Great Brain's plan so I kept quiet.

"I'm older and bigger than you," Tom continued, "but according to my father you should be able to beat me at Indian squaw wrestling. You either aren't trying or you don't believe my father."

"I tried, honest I did," Andy protested.

"Then you didn't try hard enough," Tom said. "You've

159

got to keep telling yourself that your right leg is twice as strong as any boy in town your age. Now, let's try again."

They took their positions lying on their backs. Again Tom counted. At the count of three they locked legs. They began to grunt and strain. I couldn't believe my eyes as I watched Andy slowly force Tom's leg down and keel my brother over in a somersault.

"You did it!" Tom shouted as he pounded Andy on the back.

"You mean I won fair and square?" Andy asked as if he couldn't believe it.

"Fair and square," Tom said, "but you need a lot of practice. We'll put in one hour of practice every day until you are the best Indian squaw wrestler in town."

Andy was whistling for the first time since he'd lost his leg as he left our barn an hour later. I asked Tom if Andy had really won most of the matches that afternoon.

"No, J.D.," Tom said, "but he thinks he did and that is what counts. I've got to build up his confidence."

At the end of two weeks daily practice Tom pronounced Andy ready to meet all comers at Indian squaw wrestling.

"The next thing is to prove you can play any game as good as a kid with two legs," Tom announced in the barn after school that day. "We'll start with Duck on a Rock."

I helped Tom carry two flat slabs of rock into the barn and place them ten paces apart. We put a round rock about the size of a baseball on each slab. We laid six round rocks about the size of a baseball near one of the slabs. Tom picked one up. The idea of the game was to knock the rock representing the duck off the slab. Tom threw and hit the duck, knocking it off. I ran to put it back.

160

Andy then made an underarm pitch and missed the slab by three feet.

"It's no good," he said, discouraged. "I can't balance myself right with this peg leg."

"Take it off," Tom said.

I watched Tom strap the peg leg to his left knee. Tom took a few steps around on the peg leg. Then he tried pitching rocks at the duck on a rock with his left leg in front of him. Then he tried pitching with his right leg in front of him.

"You get off balance," Tom said to Andy, "when you put the peg leg in front and bring your weight down on it when you pitch."

"But that is the way I pitch," Andy protested. "I can't pitch with my right leg in front."

"Of course you can," Tom said. "Now watch me."

Tom took a pitch. He missed the duck on a rock but did hit the slab. He took off the peg leg and handed it to Andy.

"Now we'll play," Tom said. "The first one to knock the duck off the rock ten times is the winner."

The first game Tom got ten ducks before Andy knocked off even one. The second game Andy improved. He got two ducks before Tom knocked off ten. They kept at it until it was time for Andy to go home. During the last game Andy knocked off five ducks before Tom got ten.

"Practice makes perfect," Tom said as we came out of the barn. "We'll keep at it until you can hold your own with any kid in town."

The next afternoon after school when Andy met us in the barn, his face was thoughtful.

"I wish you'd do something about my chores," he said to

161

Tom. "My pa is going to think I'm useless as long as he has to do my chores for me."

"I guess that is more important than learning how to play games with your peg leg," Tom said. "We'll spend half our time each day teaching you how to do your chores and the other half teaching you how to play games. Now, why can't you do your chores?"

"Well, gee," Andy said, "you know I've got a peg leg."

"Answer the question," Tom said.

"Well, for one thing, I can't get up and down the back porch steps without holding on to the railing with one hand. So I can't carry an armful of kindling which you have to hold with both hands. And the bucketsful of coal are so heavy I have to lift them up the steps with both hands. And I wobble so much I can't carry a pail of milk without—"

"That's enough," Tom interrupted him. "Let's go to our back porch."

We walked to the steps of our back porch.

"Show me how you go up and down the steps," Tom ordered Andy.

Andy took hold of the railing and walked up and down the steps.

"Take off the peg leg and let me try it," Tom said. "You try to go up and down as if you had two good legs. When you put the peg leg up first, you have to pull yourself up by holding on to the railing."

Tom strapped on the peg leg. "Now watch me," he said.

He put his right foot on a step and using his right leg lifted his body up, bringing the peg leg up beside his right leg. "There is nothing to it," he said. "Let your good right leg do all the work."

162

Andy watched bug-eyed as Tom went up the rest of the steps without holding on to the railing.

"Now I'll come down," Tom said.

He tried putting his right foot down first and lost his balance. He had to grab the railing to keep from falling.

"It worked going up," Tom said.

Again he tried putting his right foot down first. Again he lost his balance. He sat down on the steps.

"If it works going up, why won't it work going down?" he asked as if talking to himself. "You fellows be quiet. I've got to put my great brain to work."

Andy and I remained quiet. I knew Tom's great brain was working like sixty as I watched wrinkles come into his forehead. Suddenly the wrinkles disappeared. Tom was smiling as he stood up.

"I used my good leg to lift my body going up," he said. "I made the mistake of trying to use the peg leg to lift my body going down. Now watch this."

Tom balanced himself on his right leg, holding his weight as he put the peg leg down a step. Then he stood on the peg leg for just a second while he quickly brought his right foot down a step. He came like that all the way down the steps without losing his balance. He took off the peg leg and handed it to Andy.

"You saw me go up using my right leg to lift my body and you saw me come down using my right leg to lift my body," he said. "Now you try it."

Andy strapped on the peg leg. He had no trouble going up but lost his balance coming down.

"It is harder to come down," Tom said, "but don't get discouraged. All it takes is practice."

163

Tom made Andy practice going up and down the steps for an hour.

The next afternoon after school Tom and I were waiting for Andy on the steps of our back porch. Again Tom made Andy go up and down the steps for an hour. Andy got so he could practically run up and down the steps without holding on to the railing.

The next afternoon Tom's face was thoughtful as we waited for Andy. "You know, J.D.," he said to me, "I think it is time for Andy to learn how to carry things up and down the steps. And to make sure he can do his chores to please his father, I think I'll start letting him do ours."

When Andy arrived, my brother led him to the wood-shed. "We are going to start practicing doing real chores today," Tom said. "We'll begin by letting you fill all the wood boxes in our house with kindling wood."

Andy looked so happy I didn't have the heart to tell him that he was being taken. With a big happy grin on his face he carried a big armful of kindling wood from our woodshed, up the steps, into the kitchen and dumped it into the wood box by the kitchen range.

"What is this all about?" Mamma asked.

"I'm teaching Andy how to do his chores," Tom said proudly.

Aunt Bertha just shook her head. "Oh, that boy," she said.

I watched as Andy filled the woodboxes for the fireplace, the pot-bellied stove in the dining room, and the stove in the bathroom.

"Now for the coal buckets," Tom said as we came out of the kitchen carrying empty coal buckets. Then I guess my brother's conscience bothered him a bit. "No hurry, Andy," he said. "Take a rest first if you want."

Andy still had that happy grin on his face. "I don't need a rest," he said. "Let's go."

After Andy had filled all the coal buckets in our house, I thought that was enough for one day. But not Tom.

"I'd let you do the milking," Tom said, "but I'm afraid you might spill it carrying it. So, we'll spend the rest of the day practicing."

Tom got a milk pail and filled it full of water at the hydrant. "Now I want you to practice carrying this to the barn and back until it is time for you to go home."

Andy spilled half the water out of the bucket the first trip as Tom and I watched.

"No wonder your father won't let you bring in the milk," Tom said. "Give me that bucket."

My brother filled the pail with water. Then he strapped on the peg leg. He picked up the pail of water and started to walk. He spilled water all over.

"Now watch, J.D.," he said, "and tell me if the water spills when I'm on my right leg or the peg leg."

I watched as Tom started to walk. The water spilled when he tried to step on the peg leg. I told him so.

"It's because I'm trying to take a natural step," he said. "Now I'm only going to take a little short step with the peg leg to help me keep an even balance."

He looked funny taking a little short step with the peg leg and a big step with the right leg, but he didn't spill a drop. He removed the peg leg and made Andy put it on while he filled the pail to the brim with water.

"Now do like you saw me do," he said to Andy. "A

165

little short step with the peg leg and a natural step with the good leg."

Tom made Andy practice until it was time for Andy to go home.

"Can I start doing my chores at home tomorrow?" Andy asked as if excited.

"No," Tom said. "You need at least another week of practice. We don't want to take any chances your father won't be completely satisfied."

Tom made Andy do all our chores for a whole week before he announced Andy could do his own chores starting the following day.

It was a proud day for Andy when he reported he had done all the chores he used to do at home before he lost his leg.

"I brought in the kindling and the coal," he said when he met us at school. "I slopped the pigs without spilling any of the slop from the buckets. I carried the milk in without spilling a drop. I fed the chickens and collected the eggs. I went to the store for Ma and carried everything home without dropping anything. Pa says he is proud of me. I guess he doesn't think I'm plumb useless anymore."

"You are still useless as a kid," Tom said. "What good is a kid who can't run? If you can't run, you can't play a lot of games. Meet me in our corral after school and I'll start teaching you to run."

"I can't stay late anymore," Andy said. "I've got my chores to do now."

"We'll only spend a half an hour a day on school days," Tom said.

Andy walked home from school with Tom and me. I knew my brother had a great brain, but trying to teach a

166

kid with a peg leg to run was beyond my imagination. I was curious as all get out as we entered the corral.

Tom ordered Andy to run around the corral. Andy tried to run but kept falling down. Then Tom strapped on the peg leg. He had no better luck than Andy and kept falling down.

"There must be some way of doing it," he said, undaunted. "Tomorrow is Saturday. Meet me here tomorrow afternoon. I'll put my great brain to work on it and figure out a way to make you run."

The next morning Tom and I did all our chores and then Mamma kept finding other things for us to do. We didn't get a chance to even sit down and rest until just before lunch. We were sitting on the swing on our front porch. We were watching Irene Olsen and Christine Mackie playing hopscotch across the street. Tom suddenly snapped his fingers.

"That's it!" he shouted.

"What?" I asked.

"My great brain has figured out a way to make Andy run!" he said, grinning.

"How?" I asked, wondering how a kid with a peg leg could ever learn to run.

"You'll see this afternoon," Tom said mysteriously.

We ate lunch and then went to meet Andy in our corral. He arrived a few minutes later.

"Give me that peg leg," Tom said.

Tom strapped on the peg leg.

"Now watch this!" he shouted.

I burst out laughing as Tom took a hop, skip, and jump on his right leg and then a step on the peg leg. It was like watching a man run on three legs and looked very comical. He fell down a few times but kept on trying until he'd run all the way across the corral and back without even stumbling.

"Now you try it," Tom said to Andy as he unstrapped the peg leg.

An hour later and Andy was ready to give up. He kept falling down when he tried to run.

"It's no good," he said, "and besides my knee hurts."

"How do you think my knee feels?" Tom demanded as he rolled up his pants leg and showed us a knee that was turning black and blue. "My great brain has figured out a way to make you run and you're going to learn how to run. Now try it again."

A week later Andy was singing a different tune. Tom had made him practice running every day.

"Today," Tom said as we entered the corral, "you are going to race J.D. across the corral and back and you are going to beat him."

"I'll beat him," Andy said confidently.

Andy and I got on our marks and got set. Tom gave the signal. I beat Andy across the corral but I had to slow down to turn around. Andy just spun around on his peg leg without slowing down and beat me back to the starting line.

"You can now run well enough to play any game," Tom announced.

"I can't play ball," Andy said.

"Why not?" Tom asked.

"Because I can't bat with a peg leg," Andy explained.

"We'll fix that," Tom said.

And fix it he did. Within a week he had Andy batting better with a peg leg than Andy could ever bat with two good legs. Tom discovered that Andy shut his eyes when he took a swing at the ball. As soon as he trained Andy to keep his eyes on the ball, Andy began whacking Tom's pitches all over the corral.

On a Friday Tom held a whispered conference with Basil during the morning recess. When school let out, Tom and I walked part of the way home with Andy.

"Tomorrow is the big day," Tom announced. "Meet me in my backyard in the morning and I'll prove you aren't useless as a kid anymore."

The three of us were in our backyard the next morning when Basil arrived with Sammy Leeds, Danny Forester, Jimmie Peterson, and Pete Kyle.

Sammy was the first to speak. "Basil tells us he is retiring as champion Indian squaw wrestler. I guess that makes you champ, Tom."

"I don't know about that," Tom said. "You almost beat me a few times."

"I almost did at that," Sammy said, nodding.

"With Basil retiring," Tom said, "I think it's only fair to hold an elimination contest to find out who the new champion is going to be."

Tom led the way around to our front lawn, which was turning brown from the approach of winter.

"As runner-up to the champ," Tom said, "it will be up to me to defeat all challengers if I'm to be the champion. Who wants to try first?"

"I'll try," Jimmie Peterson said. "I know I can't beat you but I'll try."

Tom had no trouble beating Jimmie, Danny, Pete, and me. It was then Sammy's turn. I couldn't believe my eyes as I watched Sammy win the first match. Tom came back and won the second match. The rubber match looked as if it was going to be a tie. At the count of three they locked knees.

They grunted and puffed with their right legs remaining upward for a long time. Then slowly and surely Sammy began pushing Tom's leg down. I watched with astonishment as Sammy flipped my brother over backward and won the rubber match.

Sammy jumped to his feet, grinning. "I guess that makes me champ," he said.

Tom got up looking very downhearted because he'd lost. "There is one more challenger," he said. "Andy."

"It wouldn't be fair to wrestle a cripple," Sammy said.

"You can't be the champion unless you take on all challengers," Tom said.

"I'll put him down without trying," Sammy boasted.

Sammy and Andy lay down on the lawn and took their positions. Tom counted one, two, three and they locked legs at the knees. There was a look of complete bewilderment on Sammy's face as Andy flipped the bigger boy over in a backward somersault.

"I wasn't set," Sammy complained to Tom.

"All right," Tom said. "The first one doesn't count. Now for the championship match. Best two out of three. Are you ready this time, Sammy?"

"All set," Sammy replied.

Andy won two straight matches and became the new champion. We all crowded around Andy to congratulate him and pat him on the back, except Sammy. Poor old Sammy just sat on the lawn with a look on his face as if he still couldn't believe Andy had beaten him.

Tom suggested we go into our backyard and play Duck on a Rock. Only four could play at a time. Tom chose Andy for his partner. Sammy chose Danny Forester as his partner for the first game. Tom and Andy beat Sammy and Danny.

Then they beat Basil and Jimmie and finally had no trouble beating Pete Kyle and me.

"Let's change partners this time," Sammy suggested. "I'll take Andy for my partner."

I don't know if my brother tried his best or not, but Andy and Sammy knocked off ten ducks to eight ducks for Tom and Danny and won the game. Then Sammy and Andy beat Basil and Jimmie and then clobbered me and Pete.

"I've had enough of this game," Tom said. "Let's play Kick the Can."

"Why not play something Andy can play?" Sammy asked.

"What makes you think he can't play Kick the Can?" Tom asked.

"He can't run on his peg leg," Sammy said.

"We always let J.D. play," Tom said. "If Andy can beat him running, it means he can play."

"Sure," Sammy agreed, "but how can Andy run on a peg leg?"

Tom pointed. "They will race to the end of the alley and back to the woodshed."

We all went into the alley, where Andy and I got on our marks.

"One for the money," Tom chanted, "two for the show, three to get on your marks, and off you go."

I ran as fast as I could, but Andy beat me back to the woodshed by ten feet.

"Gosh, Peg Leg," Sammy said, patting Andy on the shoulder, "you were just great. I would never have believed it if I hadn't seen it with my own eyes." He began laughing. "You looked funny as the devil, but how you can run."

The other kids all congratulated Andy. We played Kick the Can until it was time for lunch. I had to run an errand for Mamma after lunch. I ran all the way to the Smiths' vacant lot after the errand where I knew the kids were meeting to play baseball. Tom and Sammy had just finished hands over fists on Sammy's bat. Tom had won and got first choice in choosing up the two teams to play. Sammy didn't even look surprised when Tom chose Andy first. I guess after what had happened that morning Sammy wouldn't have been surprised if Andy had run and jumped over our barn.

We knew we would have time to play only five innings before we all had to go home and do our chores. I was playing third base on Tom's team. My brother was pitching and Andy was catching. Tom held our opponents scoreless for four innings, but in the top of the fifth they got two runs before we made the third out. Tom was lead-off man our last time at bat. He hit the second pitch for a single. Basil then made a sacrifice bunt that put Tom on second base. Then Sammy, who was pitching, got wild and gave Pete Kyle a base on balls. Sammy settled down and struck out Seth Smith. It was then Andy's turn at bat and our only hope of winning the game. He took two strikes and two balls and then hit the next pitch for a home run. We won the game three to two.

It had taken Tom and his great brain four weeks to prove Andy wasn't useless and could hold his own in any games we kids played. I'd forgotten about the erector set until after supper that evening. Andy came to our front door carrying the set under his arm. He asked Tom to come out on the front porch. I followed.

"Here is the erector set like I promised," Andy said. "I told my pa all you did for me. I told him how you showed me I could still do my chores with my peg leg. I told him how you helped me so I could play games with the kids with my peg leg. I told him how you made me feel I was no longer useless. I told him how I would have killed myself if it hadn't been for you. I told him how you made me want to go on living. And I told him I had promised you the erector set if you could prove to him and to me I wasn't useless anymore. Pa said it was all right to give it to you."

It was at that moment in my brother's life when he was suddenly attacked by a strange disease which completely paralyzed his great brain and he didn't know what he was saying or doing. At least that is what I thought when Tom didn't snatch the erector set out of Andy's hands.

"It is true," Tom said modestly. "My great brain saved you from a suicide's grave. It is also true I proved to you and your pa that you weren't useless. And it is true we made a deal and I have more than lived up to my end of the bargain. But it just doesn't seem right somehow for me to take the erector set."

Andy's eyes got wide. "Don't you want it?" he asked, hugging the set to his chest.

"Of course I want it," Tom answered, "but it just doesn't seem right getting paid for helping somebody not to be useless anymore. You keep the set, Andy. I'll come over and play with it sometimes."

It is a dream, I told myself. I watched Andy press his lips together as tears bubbled up in his eyes.

"You can play with the set anytime," he said. "And my pa said to thank you for him. My ma said God bless you and she would pray for you. Ain't no way for me to say what I feel inside for you making me so I'm not useless anymore. I guess I'll just have to thank you in my prayers and ask God to bless you too."

Andy walked to our front gate. I could see tears stream-

173

ing down his cheeks as he turned to wave at us. I knew they were tears of happiness and gratitude as I watched him go whistling down Main Street with the erector set under his arm. Then my thoughts turned to my poor brother.

"I'll get Mamma to call Dr. LeRoy right away," I said, starting for the front door, positive my poor brother was so sick he didn't know what he was doing.

Tom grabbed my arm and stopped me. "I'm not sick, J.D.," he said, smiling at me. "As a matter of fact I feel extra good inside. Sort of clean and warm and Christmasy."

I stood there bug-eyed as I watched Tom remove the Indian beaded belt Uncle Mark had given me for my birthday and hold out the belt toward me.

"Here is your belt back, J.D.," he said. "It is a little worn by now but still the only genuine Indian beaded belt in town."

There wasn't anything my brother could have done to convince me more that he expected to die any moment from this strange malady that had seized him.

"I'm not going to take advantage of you when I know you are so sick you don't know what you are saying or doing," I said with my heart breaking with pity for my poor brother.

"Please, J.D.," Tom said as he pleaded with me for the first time in his life, "if you love me as a brother you will take back the belt. I'm not sick. I give you my word. It is just that something has come over me and made me feel real good inside."

And so it came to pass just a week before Christmas of that year a miracle took place in Adenville, Utah. The Christmas spirit arrived at our house early and with the help of a boy with a peg leg made a true Christian out of my brother.

174

Things got mighty dull after The Great Brain decided to give up his crooked ways and to walk the straight and narrow. So dull Papa didn't even bother to come upstairs and see if Tom was in bed the night the schoolhouse burned down. So dull there is no more to tell.

About the Author

John D. Fitzgerald was born in Utah and lived there until he was eighteen, when he left to be a drummer with a jazz band. Since then he has worked for an advertising agency and has been a newspaperman, a foreign correspondent, a purchasing agent, and a bank auditor. But whatever his occupation, he has always loved to write.

Mr. Fitzgerald has written a textbook, numerous short stories and articles, and three novels for adults: *Papa Married a Mormon, Mamma's Boarding House,* and *Uncle Will and the Fitzgerald Curse.* His novels have been translated into several languages, and *Papa Married a Mormon* was a runaway best seller. Mr. Fitzgerald and his wife now live in Denver. *The Great Brain* is his first book for young people.